DEVIL AT THE GATES

A Gothic Romance

LAUREN SMITH

Copyright © 2020 by Lauren Smith

A Gentleman Never Surrenders excerpt Copyright © 2015 by Lauren Smith

*This story was previously published in the limited run boxed set *A Lady's Christmas Rake*.

ISBN: 978-0-9974237-0-9 (e-book edition)

ISBN: 978-1-947206-35-9 (print edition)

PROLOGUE

DOVER, ENGLAND · 1793

The Duke of Frostmore stirred fitfully in his bed. The sheets that clung to his skin were damp and fresh with terrible dreams that had jolted him awake. He'd never slept well when it rained, even as a boy when he'd simply been known as Redmond Barrington. There was something about the sound, the way it plinked against the windows as the wind whined through the cracks in the stones of the large old medieval manor house.

He rubbed his eyes and squinted at the darkened bedchamber. Something had awoken him, something outside his door. A soft cry came, echoing through the gloom. Redmond turned in his bed to see if his wife had been disturbed. But the bed was cold, empty.

The duchess was gone.

He shoved back the covers and pulled on his dressing gown.

"Millicent?" He wondered if she'd perhaps gone to her bedroom, which was next door. He'd agreed to the tradition of allowing his wife to have a separate room, but he'd told her from the start that he longed to share his bed each night with her. She'd been hesitant, like many a new bride, but he'd cajoled her into agreeing at last to share in the intimacy of remaining in his bed after they'd made love. Whatever had drawn her from his bed tonight? Had she fallen somewhere, gotten hurt while walking in the dark?

The stones beneath his feet were ice cold, but he didn't mind. He liked the cold, liked the way it stirred his senses and kept him alert. He cracked open his bedchamber door and peered out into the corridor. The sound came again, but he saw nothing to indicate where it was coming from. He eased farther into the hall, still listening. Finally, he traced the sound to a bedchamber down the hall, the one belonging to his younger brother, Thomas.

"Thomas?" Redmond rapped at the door and pressed his ear to listen. There was a rush of hushed voices, followed by silence. Redmond's heart fluttered as his mind made the terrible connection as to his missing wife and the voices coming from his brother's room.

"Red?" Thomas finally asked as he opened the bedroom door. His hair was mussed, and he was only half-dressed. "What are you doing up? It's late..."

"Are you alone? I heard a crying sound. I'm worried Millicent is hurt. She wasn't in bed when I awoke. Will you help me find her?"

Thomas swallowed hard, and his gaze darted to the left as he began to craft a lie. Redmond had practically raised his younger brother and knew right away when Thomas wasn't being truthful. Which meant...he knew where Millicent was.

Redmond's heart hardened as he faced the betrayal by his own blood.

"She's with you, isn't she?" Redmond's veins filled with ice as he spoke what he hadn't wanted to admit had been true for months.

It hadn't been a cry of pain he'd heard but one of *passion*. A sound he'd never been able to coax from his wife since they'd married six months ago. She'd remained gentle and still beneath him in bed, and each time he'd tried and failed to excite her. Most of the time, he'd given up and rolled away from her, his heart pained by his failure.

Thomas's eyes refused to meet his. "She is."

Redmond kept his rage reined in, but barely. He loved his brother, but Thomas was a fool who would follow his heart right into the bed of a married woman, even the wife of his own brother.

"Redmond, please...let me explain," Thomas began again, but unable to find the words, he sighed and stepped back, letting Redmond enter the room.

Millicent peered around the edge of the changing screen in the corner of the room, her eyes wide with fear.

"Millicent." Redmond spoke her name softly, and even that gave a stab of pain to his chest.

"I'm sorry," she whispered. He saw the truth glimmering in her pretty blue eyes as they filled with tears. "I love him, Red. I think I've always loved him."

"Yet you accepted my proposal?" Redmond rubbed at his temples as a headache began to pound the backs of his eyelids. How had he been so bloody blind to let this slip of a young woman fool him into thinking she cared about him? Because he'd wanted to be loved, to be cherished for himself and not his title.

"My father said I had to accept you...to have a duchess in the family. He...he was so proud of me." The words trembled on her lips.

Thomas stepped between them. His stance was casual, but Redmond knew his brother was ready to protect Millicent should he fly into a rage. But the rage that brewed inside him was not directed at her. The pretty young woman was only nineteen, married to him less than six months and clearly too young to make a decision that would affect the rest of her life. No, Redmond was furious with himself. He was twenty-five, old enough to know he should have sensed Millicent's attraction to his title and not to him.

My damnable pride, he thought darkly.

Redmond walked over to the crackling fire in the hearth and braced one hand on the marble mantel. His thoughts raced wildly until they jerked to a halt. He turned around to face the exposed couple. Thomas had his arm around the girl's shoulders, and tears streamed down her face.

"You want Thomas?" he finally asked. Each word cost him much to even speak. A world-weary sorrow began to leach into his anger, eating away at him until he felt nothing at all. He was as hollow as the old dead trees in the woods beyond his estate.

Millicent nodded, the girlish hope in her gaze only deepening the emptiness inside him. She'd never looked at him that way, with hope.

"Then I give you my blessing. I will contact my solicitor tomorrow. We will have to demand an annulment which won't be easy. But know this—once this is settled, neither of you must return here ever again." He couldn't bear to see them, even his beloved brother. The pain would be too great. To annul a marriage meant he'd never consummated his love for his wife, but he had. Everything was built upon more lies now.

Thomas's lips parted as though he wished to speak, but then he seemed to reconsider and answered with a nod.

"Thank you, Redmond... I...," Millicent started, but her words died as Redmond stared at her.

"Don't," he warned before she could say another word. Redmond stalked from the room. He could not stand to listen to her thank him for letting her break his heart.

He didn't go back to bed. There would be no sleeping now. He headed to his study and sat in the moonlit room as he retrieved a bottle of scotch from his liquor tray by his desk. He didn't bother with the glasses. He simply drank from the bottle until his stomach revolted and he choked on the liquid. Then he leaned back in his chair and stared out the tall bay window overlooking the road that led to the cliffs. The sea would be harsh this time of year, the fall winds giving way to icy winter. He could simply go, walk out into the night and head to the cliffs. No one would see. No one would stop him. No one would care.

Thomas would become the Duke of Frostmore, and all would be well. Thomas had always been the favorite, the more handsome, more charming, more likable brother. He'd heard the whispers all his life: *Why couldn't Thomas have been born the first son?* Even his own parents had preferred Thomas. Redmond was quiet, intense, gruff at times, and not everyone understood him. Now it had cost him what little happiness he had carved out for himself.

Why had he ever thought Millicent would choose him when Thomas was at his side? From the moment he'd met the girl, her laughs had been for Thomas, her smiles, even her cries of passion. Redmond had never stood a chance.

Because I wanted to be loved, fool that I am.

He stared out at the cliffs a long time before he made a decision. A divorced man would have few options—no decent woman would ever be enticed by his title to become a second duchess after such a scandal broke. There was only one way to end this. He rose from his chair and grasped the bottle of scotch, taking another long, burning swallow.

"I never wished to be a bloody duke anyway," he muttered as he walked unsteadily out the door of Frostmore, his ancestral home. "Good riddance."

He stumbled a little but kept walking toward the cliffs until he could hear the crashing sound of the waves. There was nothing more beautiful or haunting than the sea when she was angry. Rain lashed his face and blinded his eyes to all but the lightning splitting the skies overhead. He moved numbly across the cold grass until he felt the rocky ledge was beneath his feet, and he wavered at the edge, his breath coming fast and his head spinning from grief and alcohol. All he wanted in that moment was for it to be over, to lose himself in the dark violence of the sea below. Then he took that final step toward the craggy abyss...

FAVERSHAM, ENGLAND - SEVEN YEARS LATER

T he bedchamber in Thursley Manor was dark except for a few lit oil lamps. The wind whistled clearly through the cracks in the mortar in between the stones. Harriet Russell tried to ignore the storm outside as she clutched her mother's hand. This old house, with its creaks and groans in the night, had never been a home to either of them, yet Harriet feared it would be her mother's last resting place.

"Harriet." Her mother moaned her name. Pain soaked each syllable as her mother coughed. The raspy sound tore at Harriet's heart.

Harriet brushed her other hand over her mother's forehead. "Rest, Mama." Beneath the oil lamp's glow, her mother's face was pale, and sweat dewed upon her skin as fever raged throughout her body.

"So little time," her mother said with a sigh. "I must tell you..." Harriet watched her mother struggle for words and the breath to speak. "Soon... You will be twenty. Your father..."

Harriet didn't correct her, but George Halifax had *never* been her father. No, the man who held that title had died when she was fourteen. Edward Russell had been a famous fencing master, both in England and on the continent. He'd also been a loving man with laughing eyes and a quick wit whom she missed with her whole heart.

"Yes, Mama?" She desperately needed to hear what her mother had to say.

"George is your guardian, but on your birthday, you will be free to live your life as you choose."

Free. What an amazing notion. How desperately she longed for that day to come. George was a vile man who made her skin crawl whenever she was in the same room as him, and she wished every day that her mother hadn't been desperate enough to accept his offer of marriage. But fencing masters, even the greatest ones, did not make a living that could sustain a widow and a small daughter.

"Mama, you will get better." Harriet dipped a fresh cloth in clean water and placed it over her mother's brow.

"No, child. I won't." The weary certainty in her

mother's voice tore at her heart. But they both knew that consumption left few survivors. It had claimed her father's laugh six years before, and now it would take her mother from her as well.

The bedchamber door opened, and Harriet turned, expecting to see one of the maids who had been checking on them every few hours to see if they needed anything. But her stepfather stood there. George Halifax was a tall man, with bulk and muscle in equal measures. The very sight of him chilled her blood. She'd spent the last six years trying to avoid his attentions, even locking her door every night just to be sure. She may be only nineteen, but she had grown up quickly under this man's roof and learned to fear what men desired of her.

"Ah...my dearest wife and daughter." George's tone sounded outwardly sincere, but there was the barest hint of mocking beneath it. He moved into the room, boots thudding hard on the stone. He was so different from her father. Edward had been tall and lithe, moving soundlessly with the grace of his profession in every step.

"Mother needs to rest." Harriet looked at her mother, not George, as she spoke. Whenever she met his gaze, it made her entire body seize with panic, and her instincts urged her to run.

"Then perhaps you want to leave her to rest?" George challenged softly.

Harriet raised hateful eyes to his. "I won't leave. She needs someone to look after her."

"Yes, you will leave, daughter." He stepped deeper into the room, fists clenched.

"I'm not your daughter," Harriet said defiantly. His lecherous gaze swept over her body.

"You're right. You could be so...much...more." He paused between the last three words, emphasizing what she knew he had wanted for years.

"George...," her mother, Emmeline, gasped. "No, please..."

"Hush, my dear. You need your rest. Harriet and I shall have a little talk outside. About her future." He came toward her, but Harriet moved fast, despite the hampering nature of her simple gown. She'd been trained by the best to never be caught flat-footed.

"Stop!" George snarled and grabbed her by the skirts as she ducked under his arm. With a sudden jerk, she hit the ground, her left shoulder and hip hitting the pine floorboards hard. A whimper escaped her as he dragged her to her feet and slapped her across the face.

Her mother made a soft sound of distress from the bed, and she heard the whisper as though from a vast distance away.

"Harriet...go...*run!*"

Harriet kicked George in the groin as hard as she could. He released her to clutch himself.

"Get her!" George shouted in rage.

Two hulking men she didn't recognize from among the household staff of Thursley Manor rushed into the room. She tried to dodge them, but they trapped her in the corner and dragged her from the room by her arms.

"Lock her up!" George's shout followed them down the corridor.

Her mother called out weakly for her, but no matter how Harriet screeched and fought, they wouldn't let go. She was taken to an empty bedroom and shoved inside. The door was locked with a clack of cold iron. Shivering hard, her shoulder and hip still sore from her fall, Harriet threw herself at the door, but she was too small to break the sturdy oak.

Her mother's warning had come too late. She wouldn't turn twenty for another month, and George was already taking control of her, just as she feared he would. There was nothing he couldn't do to her, stranded as she was at Thursley. They were too far from the town of Faversham for anyone to come this way except on purpose. She had no friends, no one who would worry about her, which she now suspected with dread was what George had wanted all along.

The dark bedchamber was bracing in its chill. No fire had been lit in the small hearth, and she knew no one would come to see to the task. There was only one small oil lamp on the side table next to the bed. She dug around in the drawers of the side table until she found a pair of steel strikers. She used the strikers to light the lamp. The light blossomed into a healthy glow, but it offered no warmth. Outside the storm seemed to build as rain joined the howling winds.

She had to escape. Harriet attempted to pry the windows open, but nails were driven deep into the wooden frames. She even studied the lock of the door, trying to use a hairpin to see if she could twist the tumblers in a way that would set her free, but nothing worked.

A few hours later, footsteps echoed in the corridor. A key jangled in the lock, and a latch lifted. She tensed, her muscles tightening as she expected to see her stepfather or one of his men. But she saw only the cook, Mrs. Reed.

"Thank God you're all right, lass." The tall Scottish woman placed one hand on her bosom. "I was worried to death when I found out he had locked you up." Mrs. Reed spoke in a whisper and glanced down the darkened hall behind her, as though fearful of being overheard.

"Mrs. Reed... My mother... Is she...?" Harriet choked on the words.

"No, not yet, lass, but there's no time. You must go. *Now*." The cook came into the room and cupped her face the way Harriet's mother used to. "I know you dinna want to go, but you must."

"I can't leave Mama here, not with him."

"You can and you will. Your mother told me when she fell ill that she feared she wouldna be around to protect you. She made me promise that I'd help you escape," Mrs. Reed insisted. "The master has plans for you. Plans I cannot abide, you ken. He means to hurt you, to use you like a..." She shook her head as though the rest of what she might have said was too awful. "He wanted me to drug you. But I drugged him and his men instead. We dinna have long." The cook put an arm around her shoulders and dragged her back down the servants' stairs and into the kitchens. A scullery maid named Bess was cleaning a pot and looked up at them as they entered.

"How are they, lass?" Mrs. Reed asked the girl.

"Still asleep," Bess whispered, her eyes wide with fear. "Mr. Johnson has the coach ready. He thinks he can take Miss Russell as far as Dover, despite the storm."

"Dover?" Harriet repeated in shock. That was so far away.

"Aye, lassie. You'll take this." Mrs. Reed pulled a leather pouch of coins from a pocket in her dress. "Buy passage to Calais."

"France?" Harriet trembled. To travel alone as a single woman was to invite trouble, possibly even danger.

"France will be safe. The master could have you tracked from here all the way to the bloody Isle of Skye in the north. 'Tis best if you leave England."

Harriet swallowed hard and nodded. She knew some French and could learn more when she was there. Her father had relatives in Normandy, second cousins. Perhaps she could reach them and find work. She tried to do what her mother had taught her, which was to focus on a plan of action rather than let fear freeze her in place.

Mrs. Reed pulled a heavy woolen cloak off of a nearby coatrack and wrapped it around her shoulders. "We have no time to delay." She led Harriet to the servants' entrance, which took them to the back of the house where the stables were. George's coach stood waiting, and the driver huddled near the horses, which pawed the ground uncertainly.

The rain came down in thick sheets, and Harriet splashed through the mud to the waiting coach.

"Take this." Mrs. Reed followed her and handed

her a basket of food before she climbed into the vehicle.

"Mrs. Reed..." There were a thousand things she wanted to say, and a dozen new fears assailed her at what her life would become now as she fled. But only one thing truly mattered above all the rest. Her mother was still dying, and Harriet was abandoning her.

"I know, lass." The cook squinted in the rain and squeezed her hand. "I know, but you canna stay here." She turned to head back to the servants' entrance.

"Take care of my mother. Tell her I made it to a ship and sailed for Calais," Harriet called out from the coach as Mr. Johnson, the driver, shut the door, sealing her inside. She wanted her mother to believe she had escaped, even if she never made it. It might be the last comfort anyone could give her. Harriet's bottom lip trembled, and she fought off a sob.

Mrs. Reed waved at her and then ducked back inside the house. Harriet began to shake as the wet woolen cloak weighed her down. An extra chill settled into her skin from her soaked clothes.

The coach jerked forward, and the basket of food in Harriet's lap nearly toppled over. She set it down on the floor and closed her eyes, trying to calm herself.

"Oh, Mama... I wish I didn't have to leave you."

But if she had stayed, the horrors she would have endured were unthinkable. And to suffer a life trapped beneath George's control... She knew he wouldn't honor her twentieth birthday—that must have been what her mother wished to tell her. That she would be free of him as a guardian, but she would need to escape him before he could stop her. Harriet collapsed back onto the seat and silently sobbed for her mother, for the life of the last person she'd loved in the world.

"Dry your eyes, kitten." Her father's voice seemed to drift from the past as old memories of her childhood came to her. She closed her eyes, imagining how he used to find her when she'd fallen and scraped a knee. He'd curl his fingers under her chin and gently make her look up into his smiling, tender face.

"Papa," she breathed, feeling more like a child now than she had for years. She clung to the vision of him inside her head.

"You are my daughter. You do not cower when life becomes difficult. Face every challenge with courage, and refuse to accept defeat."

Harriet's eyes flew open as she thought for a moment that she felt a caress on her cheek. But the ghost of him vanished just as quickly as it had come. She wiped her eyes and tried to steady herself, lest she burst into tears again.

She remembered how her father used to counsel the young lords he taught fencing. Harriet used to hide behind a tall potted plant, tucking her skirt up under her knees as she watched her father move about the large room with a dozen young men wielding fencing foils. He would call out the positions, and the men would fall in line, raising their blades and performing. When they began to tire, he would call out, *"Clear eyes, steady hands, you shall not fail."*

She would need that advice and more to find a new life in Calais.

She leaned against the wall of the coach, listening to the rain and wondering what the dawn would bring.

2

Rain whipped at the coach windows as Harriet attempted to catch a few hours of sleep. Thunder shook the road so hard that more than once Harriet was jostled awake in fright. She rubbed her eyes, fatigue hanging heavy in her limbs. It was close to midnight, and they still had a ways to go before they reached Dover. In good weather it would take at least two hours, but with the roads muddied and visibility hampered, that time might double.

With a quiet sigh, she wrapped her black wool cloak tight about her shoulders; it was freezing in the carriage. Her toes were already numb and her fingers icy as she twisted them beneath her skirts to try to keep them warm. She turned her thoughts to what would happen when she reached Calais. Harriet was completely alone and had no one to help her find her way, but surely with her passable French she could find a coach to Normandy. With the coins Mrs. Reed had given her, she should be able to afford a room at an inn before she journeyed ahead.

Caution would be crucial, however, because she knew she would be a target for men. Alone, and just shy of destitution, she would be easy prey if she wasn't careful. Harriet's only hope now was to trespass on the kindness of her father's distant cousins until she could find suitable work. She'd attended a finishing school for young ladies until her father had died, and she'd been a prized pupil of the instructors there. Perhaps she could find her way as a governess? If that didn't work, she might have a chance to be a seamstress. She wasn't completely useless with a needle and thread.

The storm only worsened as midnight passed, and the rains flooded the road. More than once, Mr. Johnson slowed the coach to allow the horses to walk through deeper pools of water that had gathered on the road. Harriet pressed her forehead against the coach window and peered into the darkness. She glimpsed nothing until a flash of lightning lit up the roads, and she was at last able to see what obstacles the horses were facing.

The poor beasts, they were risking their lives to save hers. They didn't even have the comfort of stopping here, because the countryside around Dover wasn't a safe place, at least according to the gossip she'd heard in Thursley Manor.

Harriet prayed that they would make it to Dover's harbor without a reason to stop. They were passing through the Duke of Frostmore's country, and Harriet feared meeting up with him. Redmond Barrington was known as the Dark Duke or the Devil of Dover by the servants at Thursley, and rumors followed his name like shadows cast by gravestones.

Harriet knew all the stories, of course. The duke feasted on naughty children who did not abide by the wishes of their parents; he stole the virtue of unsuspecting maidens foolish enough to travel alone in his lands. Perhaps the most gruesome tale was that he had killed his younger brother, Thomas Barrington, in a duel after Lord Frostmore discovered his brother bedding his new bride. They said he cast his wife off the cliffs before he shot Thomas in the stomach and watched him slowly bleed to death. Harriet knew that the younger brother was in fact dead, according to parish records, but no one knew the truth of how he'd met his end other than that he had been shot.

George had often bragged at dinner that he was well acquainted with Lord Frostmore, and that only made Harriet's fears of being caught in Dover that much stronger. What if the duke discovered she was here and returned her to George?

Regardless of the veracity of the grim tales, Harriet knew it was not wise to be caught alone on the duke's lands, especially when the cliffs of Dover were so close. Flights of imagination led Harriet toward visions of carriages plummeting over the cliffs and crashing into the sea below.

She shuddered at the notion of gasping for air and breathing in only icy seawater. Harriet tried to dismiss her fears as much as she could, and instead focused on thoughts of her father. She was almost asleep again when the carriage suddenly lurched and toppled onto its side.

Harriet's head struck the wall of the coach when the carriage overturned, and something warm began to trickle into her eyes. For a long moment she was paralyzed with pain and confusion as her vision blurred. Finally, her sight cleared enough for her to get up. Her right arm felt oddly numb after a violent pain. She lay against the window of the coach, which was now pressed into the muddy ground. Broken glass cut her palms as she tried to rise, and she winced as her shoulder suddenly flared with fresh pain.

"Mr. Johnson?" she called out.

There was a cry, muffled beneath the crash of thunder. Harriet shoved at the door above her so she could climb out of the side of the carriage, now the ceiling. Her hem tore as she jumped from the carriage, and her arm twinged as she braced herself to land. She sank almost instantly into several inches of oozing mud. The road was dark; moonlight was unable to pierce the storm clouds. In a brief flash of lightning, she saw Mr. Johnson clutching his leg, his face twisted in pain. Harriet ran over to him, hunching over to get a better look.

"Are you able to ride, Mr. Johnson?"

"Afraid not, Miss Russell." Mr. Johnson winced as he tried to stand, but fell back to the ground. "You should take a horse, ride to find help. I'll stay with the coach."

"We have to get you to a doctor," Harriet insisted. Lightning tore across the sky, and in the distance a mountainous edifice was momentarily revealed. "What place is that, Mr. Johnson?" She pointed in the direction of the distant building.

The driver's face darkened. "That is Lord Frostmore's estate."

"The Dark Duke?" Harriet's heart jumped in her chest.

"Yes, miss. I know you to be a brave lady, but you mustn't go there." Mr. Johnson grasped her arm as though to prevent her from going for help.

Harriet pried his fingers off her arm gently. "Is there nowhere else close enough to reach?"

"Not in this weather," the driver admitted.

"Then I must go to the duke."

"Miss, please...," the driver protested, but she shook her head.

"Do not worry about me, Mr. Johnson. Now come, let me help you up. You can rest inside the carriage until help arrives. You mustn't catch a chill in this storm."

Harriet forced him up and got him inside the carriage with some difficulty. After Mr. Johnson was secured, Harriet loosed one of the horses and pulled herself up onto the beast's back, grasping the long reins. She hadn't ridden a horse since she was a child, and while she was uncertain as to her skill now, she knew Mr. Johnson depended on her.

Her torn and muddied skirts split easily as she straddled the horse. Wrapping the reins tight around her fingers, she kicked the horse's sides. It didn't need any other urging to fly across the soaked road toward the distant estate. Her cloak flew out behind her as she dug her muddy boots into the horse's flanks again, spurring it toward the dark, shadowy edifice she'd glimpsed moments before.

Harriet rode the horse hard all the way to the gates. The heavy wrought-iron structure was open just enough for her horse to pass, but Harriet lingered at the entrance, taking in the sharp spiked tops of the gates and the stone carved with the name of "FROSTMORE" near the gates.

A pair of devilish gargoyles crouched menacingly on either side of the entrance pillars. And when the lightning flashed over them, Harriet nearly screamed as she swore they moved. More pain lanced through her shoulder, and she cried out, clutching her injured shoulder.

The large mansion lay in the gloom beyond. There within its walls was the Dark Duke. Could she pass these gates and brave the risks? Harriet thought of Mr. Johnson and his injuries, and she remembered her father's fencing lessons. She was capable of defending herself if it came to it, assuming he wasn't like her stepfather, with men hired to trap her, so she spurred her horse again and rode through the gates, ready to risk her life in order to help her driver. But she would do her best to beg for help from the servants who would answer the door, and hopefully they wouldn't share with their master that she was here. It was a small hope, but she clung to it, none-theless.

The manor house was dark; only a few lights were lit near the main entrance. She abandoned her horse and ran up the stone steps, beating on the heavy oak door with the knocker. After a few minutes, a middle-aged man with a somber face opened the door. He was in his nightclothes, with a candle raised near his head. His bleary eyes focused on her in surprise and confusion.

"Please, sir. My coachman is injured. Our carriage overturned on the road to Dover. He cannot walk or ride without assistance!" Harriet blurted out quickly.

The man took in her dirty, drenched appearance and opened the door wider. "Come in, my child. Quickly now," the man whispered in a soft tone. Harriet followed him, and he led her through dark-ened halls until they reached a small sitting room. The man lit fresh kindling under the logs in the hearth with his candle and turned to her.

"Now, more slowly, tell me exactly what has happened." He gestured for her to sit on the settee. She did her best to recount the accident on the road.

"I will see to his retrieval and care at once. Please remain here. Do not leave this room—it is better that no one but myself and a few others know you are here," the old man warned. There was a shadow of concern in his eyes that urged her compliance. He must wish to hide her arrival from the duke, and that was quite fine with her. But if the carriage was broken, she had no way to reach the port of Dover... and George may already be looking for her.

After the butler left her alone, Harriet stood up and walked to the fire, holding her hands out to warm them over the meager flames. Her shoulder still ached with a dull, agonizing pain, but she didn't want anyone to know she'd been hurt. Weakness in a woman traveling alone was even more dangerous.

A few minutes of dead silence passed with nothing but the ticking of a grandfather clock before she heard a stirring in the hall. She looked up to see a large black dog standing in the doorway. The silhouette of the creature was startling, like the interruption of a dream by a hellhound. It let out a low growl, its white teeth bared. It was nearly as tall as her chest. The dog took a step toward her, its growl deepening to a deadlier tone.

Harriet brushed her hood back and shoved wet locks of blonde hair away from her face so she could better make eye contact. Her stepfather had several mean-spirited hounds back at Thursley, which she'd had to defend herself against more than once. She did not back away or show fear. She braced her hands on her hips and leaned menacingly toward the dog. The dog took another step forward, its brown eyes boring into her blue ones. It let out a snarl and trotted toward her.

"Sit!" Harriet shouted in a commanding tone.

The massive dog froze, the growl dying in its throat. In mild confusion, it slowly lowered its back haunches so it now sat two feet away from her. For a long moment she continued to glare at the beast, which as she got a better look at it appeared to be some kind of hound...a schnauzer? But she had never seen one this large. It had a noble black beard, a strong and well-formed body, and a glossy coat.

Harriet carefully extended her hand to the creature, who craned its neck forward, brushing its wet black nose over her fingertips in a cautious but friendly manner. It snuffled loudly but made no move to bite her as she stroked its great head. The hairs on the back of her neck rose, and a sense of being watched prickled along her skin, sending little tremors down her spine.

"You are the first person Devil hasn't bitten upon first meeting," a cold voice said from the doorway.

Harriet's head flew up, and she saw a tall man leaning in the doorway. His head was afire with deep-red hair that was cut a tad too long, and his hazel eyes gleamed with the fire's distant glow like topaz. His face was carved with perfect masculinity, but there was a hint of cruelty that hung about his sensuous lips, and anger radiated from his eyes. She bit her lip and tried to still the trembling of her body as she took *him* in. There was no question—this was the Duke of Frostmore.

He was not pretty, as some men tended to be. There was certainly nothing angelic about his face or form to bring forth a sense of natural charm. Instead, he seemed to exist in a singularly masculine way that made her sit up and take notice. Fear and curiosity warred with each other as she continued to stare at him.

"Devil?" It was a foolish thing to say, but no other thoughts in her mind were coherent enough to say. The effect George had on her paled in comparison to this man. Fighting George, had it come to that, would have been difficult, but she could tell with one look that attempting to resist this man would be impossible. She swallowed hard and resolved to be pleasant, but not overly so, lest he think she was a woman he could take to his bed.

"Yes, my black-haired companion here. I spent a summer in the Bavarian Alps two years ago and brought him back with me. He's a rather new breed of dog, a giant schnauzer. Devil seemed a fitting name for the brute. He's torn many a throat from a careless man and even a few careless ladies." His tone was serious, but she thought—or rather hoped—she saw the glint of teasing in his eyes, a dark, cruel teasing.

"If that is so, perhaps the fault lies not with the beast but with his master," Harriet replied, meeting his gaze with courage, despite the fact that deep within she was quivering.

He's no different than George. You can handle him.

She tried to instill within herself a sense of confidence, but her right arm ached fiercely, and her head was pounding with a headache that made even the light of the fire sear her eyes. She had dealt with men like this, the kind who took pleasure in striking fear into a woman's heart. But Harriet was not so easily shaken.

Lord Frostmore crossed his arms and leaned lazily against the doorjamb, preventing her from escaping. She felt his eyes rake over her, as if he wanted to rip her clothes clean off her body and ravage her.

But much to her surprise, the power of those eyes was enough to send a whisper of a dark, forbidden thrill through her as well, something she'd never felt before. George had only ever disgusted her when he looked at her like that, but with this man...something was different. The anger and disdain mixed with lust in the duke's eyes seemed different. And there was something else in his gaze...shadowed not by evil, but rather by pain. Pain was something she recognized all too well.

The man snapped his fingers, and Devil trotted out of the room, leaving his master and Harriet alone.

"Might I ask, Miss...," he began.

"Russell, Harriet Russell." She blurted out her real name without thinking, but it was too late. She couldn't take it back. She could only pray that if this man indeed knew George, then George would never have had a reason to discuss her, let alone call her by her name.

"Miss Russell, what are you doing in my house at this *ungodly* hour?" His lips curved upward as he said "ungodly," as though sharing some private joke. So she'd been correct in her assumption. He was the Dark Duke, the infamous Devil of Dover.

"My carriage overturned, and my driver was injured. I sought help from the man who answered the door." She took a small step back as the duke entered the room and shut the door behind him. She heard the sound of a key turning in the door before he faced her again. Harriet gripped her wounded arm to support it, while also attempting to look relaxed, lest she betray her wounded condition.

"So my man Grindle let you in, did he?" The duke leaned back against the locked door, eyeing her with increasing interest.

"Your Grace, I did not mean to intrude, but my driver is terribly injured, and the storm is worsening."

Thunder rumbled as if on cosmic cue, shaking the house around them. Harriet tried to remain calm as the duke came closer. He wore buff breeches and a loose white lawn shirt that billowed open at his chest, revealing broad shoulders and a sculpted chest so breathtaking the angels would have wept. His state of relative undress had escaped her attention while she'd been so focused on his face and his dog.

Harriet took another involuntary step back, her body warning her of the danger that emanated from him. She should not be left alone with him. Daring to look around, she tried to find a bell cord to pull that might summon a servant to protect her if her strength failed her.

"Are you all *alone* this night, Miss Russell?" The duke was only a foot from her now, peering into her eyes.

He cupped her chin, raising her face up as he studied her. She tried to retreat, but the settee was right behind her now, her calves pressed against the base of the cushions. Lord Frostmore reached up with his other hand to undo the clasp of her cloak at her throat. The thick fabric collapsed at her feet in ebony waves of coarse wool. Harriet felt suddenly naked beneath his gaze, despite the pale-pink muslin gown she wore.

"I am alone, save for my driver," she answered. He would know the truth in her eyes if she tried to lie, and she refused to be cowed by him. The duke's hand at her throat dropped slowly to her chest and then to the rising flesh of her breasts. His fingertips traced a burning line over her skin before he withdrew his hand.

"You should *never* travel my roads alone." Lord Frostmore released her chin and turned to face the fire, no longer looking at her.

"I am not afraid," Harriet declared boldly.

He chuckled softly. "You will be before this night is through." He said this to himself, as if his words were not a warning but a dark promise.

"You would not dare touch me." Harriet's tone remained steady, despite her rising concern. She wanted to convince herself that he would do her no harm, not with Mr. Grindle and the other servants as witnesses. The duke turned back to face her, a cruel kind of delight shining in his eyes.

"I would do more than *dare*, my dear. Do you not know in whose house you stand?" He returned his focus to the fire, but she knew his attention was still upon her, as though he waited for her to scream or faint dead away like some ninny of a girl.

"You are Redmond Barrington, the Duke of Frost-more." She did not think it wise to mention his other names. The duke gave a wide smile as the firelight played with shadows on his face. Had she made a mistake in coming here? But what choice did she have? She couldn't leave Mr. Johnson injured in the midst of a dangerous storm. She'd face this devil and do whatever she had to survive the night.

※ 3 ※

"Tell me, do they still call me the Dark Duke?" the duke asked her, dark amusement coloring his tone. "Or have they adopted that other name, the Devil of Dover?"

Harriet inhaled sharply as he spun to face her.

"I see that they still do. Well, my dear Miss Russell, you have crossed a dangerous threshold. You have passed through the devil's gates, as they say." He gripped her shoulders tightly.

Harriet didn't have time to react at first as he shoved her down onto the settee. But a moment later she recovered her wits and struck him across the face. He recovered quicker than she expected from the blow, and her shoulder throbbed as punishment for the effort. He caught her wrists and pinned them against the cushions of the seat.

She screamed loudly, more from pain and fear than anger. "Unhand me!" Harriet shouted. She wouldn't be able to stop him, wouldn't be able to do a bloody thing if he...

Flashes of memory, of fighting off George and his men, only made her scream louder. This man could easily do what three men had struggled to manage only hours ago. The nightmare, it seemed, wouldn't end. Exhausted, she gasped for breath as her lungs burned.

"Go ahead, scream. No one will come. This is the house of a devil, and you've strayed too far from safety." He chuckled and released her. She whimpered as pain rolled in waves through her shoulder. The duke stepped back. His eyes narrowed as she clutched her injured arm to her chest. "I couldn't have hurt you that badly—I barely touched you," he muttered, half to himself.

She closed her eyes, waiting for him to start on her again, to hurt her further, but when she opened her eyes, he was staring at her with...concern?

"You didn't... I..." she panted, breathing through the pain. "The coach overturned, as I said...and my shoulder took the brunt of the fall." Why she felt the need to explain herself she wasn't sure.

He continued to stare at her. "Why don't you come upstairs, and I'll have a look at you." He spoke so softly that she was tempted for a moment to trust him, this man who until today she'd known only by his terrifying, legendary reputation. His focus was still on her arm, and that need to trust him, to trust *someone*, started to grow. Until his eyes rose to hers and she saw the desire in his gaze. And then her father's advice to never let her guard down resurfaced.

She couldn't trust him to play the gentleman for long. The man was a devil. It was clear in his face what he desired from her.

"If you try to remove me from this room, I demand an attempt to defend myself with honor." She raised her chin and stared at him defiantly with every bit of her remaining strength.

"So...you will not submit to me if I decide to ravage you?" He seemed strangely amused at the indignation in her tone, and his own voice sounded like he was teasing, but no decent man would tease a lady about such a thing. He leaned down toward her, placing one hand on the settee and the other on her good shoulder, pinning her in place.

"Of course not! You have no right to touch me!" She struggled, trying to loosen his hold on her shoulder, but he kept her still with apparent ease. Rather than giving in to her own fear, she embraced her anger. She was a petite woman, but she was not weak.

She'd become an expert on evasion around her stepfather, but there was no evasion possible in this moment. She would have to use her wits as a weapon until she was able to get her hands on something else she could wield.

"No right? My dear Miss Russell, rights have nothing to do with this. You have trespassed into my domain. My rules govern here, no one else's." He abruptly bent to press his lips against hers in a harsh kiss. The sudden sensation overwhelmed her for a moment—the heat of his mouth, the taste of his lips, and his warm breath that made her body stir to life. A moment later, reality crashed back in on her as she felt the gentle scrape of his teeth on her lower lip. Seizing the opportunity, Harriet bit his lip, drawing blood. He jerked back with a snarl. She braced for a blow, but it never came. He released her uninjured shoulder and stepped back, glowering at her.

"Damn you, you little minx!" He licked at the blood trickling down his bottom lip. Lord Frostmore then wiped at his mouth with his fingertips. He suddenly chuckled and shook his head, then muttered something that sounded like "Serves me right, I suppose."

Harriet quivered with rage now. Rage felt so much stronger than fear, and it seemed to clear her head of the dull ringing from the pain from the accident.

Her eyes rose to the wall behind his head. Two fencing foils hung on the wall in a decorative style. If she could but reach them, she might yet fight her way out of the room. Lord Frostmore noticed her staring intently at the foils and smiled, his ill humor replaced with devilish delight. He reached up and took one off the wall, swishing it near his ankles. It seemed a careless move, but she saw the deftness with which he handled the foil. He seemed as intimately familiar with such a weapon as she was. Harriet rose from the settee and darted behind it as the duke approached her at a leisurely pace, teasingly waving the foil in the air. She needed to get to the other if she was to fight him off.

"I do not suppose you would permit me to defend myself as an equal?" she asked, her eyes darting to the second foil. Perhaps he would underestimate her and not realize her skill until it was too late—if only she could convince him to hand her the weapon.

"I will not simply hand it over. I should like to make a wager."

"A wager? On what?" She had never been the sort to frequent gambling establishments, but she was not remotely surprised that he was.

"I will give you the other foil, and if you can best

me, I will accost you no further this night. You can sleep safely, knowing the devil does not linger at your door. If I win, you come up to my bedchamber and I will take a look at your arm, whether you like it or not."

She did not trust him one inch. His eyes and smile betrayed him, but Harriet could not refuse the opportunity to gain possession of the foil.

"And the terms of this match?" she asked, wondering if there might be some devious catch in his plans.

"The first to draw blood. Just a scratch will do— no doubt as a woman you are familiar with such meager defenses."

The devil was provoking her. She was tempted to run him through instead, but if she could not make her ship to Calais by dawn, she would be surely caught and executed for murdering the duke, even if he was the devil.

"First blood? That I can agree to." She had moved around the settee now, her back to the wall with the foil as he pursued her slowly across the carpeted floor. If she'd felt better, she would have smiled. The duke didn't know she was the daughter of a renowned fencing master. He was going to lose.

Harriet spun quickly, taking advantage of the distance between them to jump up and rip the second foil off the wall with her good arm. Even though she was right-handed, her father had trained her to use both hands equally well in swordplay.

She turned just in time to deflect his first well-placed thrust. With a flick of her wrist, she changed the engagement of his blade's position and was able to shift her footing, leaving herself able to retreat back a few more steps. Harriet steadied her feet and raised her sword arm. The thrill of the fight dulled the pain in her right shoulder and arm enough to keep her moving quickly. She then took two fast steps and lunged. He parried and she danced back, just out of reach of his responding lunge.

"Someone has taught you some skill with a blade. A lover, perhaps?" He leapt for her again.

Harriet countered with a circular parry and then riposted with perfect technique, but he had anticipated that and evaded her through a classic disengage. He feinted a thrust and dodged back, only to surge forward again. She feinted this time and managed to cut through his loose shirt near his stomach, but he moved back too quickly, and she did not even graze his skin.

"Perhaps you ought to put that foil away, child, before you hurt yourself," he mocked cruelly.

"Careful, Your Grace, or next time I will slash deeper," she warned without the slightest bit of fear now. She would injure him if she had to, and damn the consequences.

His tone remained flippant. "Be serious, my dear. You would not dare do more than a scratch. Young ladies such as yourself are always so shocked to see blood."

Harriet wanted to growl, just as the giant black dog had done, but she couldn't lose her concentration. The duke seemed ready to abandon the rules as he vaulted over the settee, which she had so carefully put between them again. He stood on her crumpled cloak now, and Harriet smiled. She dove for the ground, grasped the cloak's edge, and ripped it out from under his feet. He fell onto his back, his foil rolling away from his hand as he looked up at her, astonished. He almost seemed ready to laugh with hearty amusement rather than scorn. Harriet advanced on him, blade tip poised at his throat. She forced him to look up and meet her gaze. Never in her life had she felt the thrill of having a man under her power like this, but now she understood why her father had warned his pupils to be cautious. One could be careless when one anticipated an easy victory.

"To first blood?" she asked with a wicked smile. There was something about this man, as frightening as he was, that drew out her own wickedness. A strange, wild need to prove she wouldn't stay afraid of him.

His eyes narrowed to slits. "You wouldn't dare..."

"I would do more than dare." She flung his own words back at him with far too much enjoyment. She flicked the blade's tip down, slashing his shoulder, tearing cloth and skin, but the line of blood was faint. A scratch, just as he'd said she would, but not because she feared blood—rather, out of respect for his talent with a blade. Her father had taught her much about fencing, but honoring one's opponent was one of the most important lessons.

"Your rules may govern here, but so does a sword," she added with a confident smile. She knew her father's trade well enough to keep this devil at bay. Lord Frostmore rolled up onto his feet now, brushing his pants before he looked at her again, this time more critically and with far less anger.

"It seems a sword's tip provides enough persuasion for me to offer you dinner while we await your driver's rescue and a room is prepared for you tonight. Would you permit me?" He unlocked the door and gestured for her to precede him into the hall. She kept her sword raised, expecting him to change his mind at any moment and pounce on her.

"You may go first, to show me the way." She was not foolish enough to offer him her exposed back.

The duke led her back down the hall and into a large dining room. He summoned a servant to light candles and bring wine and food. Harriet took the seat farthest from him at the opposite end of the long table, putting her foil on the edge of the table within easy reach. Her shoulder still ached fiercely, but she masked any hint of pain.

"You said that your name is Russell? You would not be kin to Edward Russell, the fencing master? Does he still teach?"

"I am his daughter. He died six years ago." She watched his hooded eyes for any reaction.

"The man was a fine tutor to many a lad at Cambridge. I am pleased he taught you his trade as well." The duke's lips twitched in a small smile. "What brings you through Dover? Your father had a home in the Cotswolds, if I remember correctly."

"We lived there before he died. I was on my way to Calais to join his family." She didn't mention her mother; even thinking of her brought such fresh pain.

"You have my condolences," the duke replied. There was a strange sincerity that seemed out of place as he said it, but it was brief, and his eyes soon glinted again with a cavalier attitude that spoke of a man who indulged in dark pleasures and cared not one whit about anyone judging him for it.

A servant entered the dining room, bearing a tray

of hastily prepared food and a bottle of wine. The duke ate immediately and without concern, sampling all of the dishes as though to show her he had no intention of poisoning her. Harriet was famished after the long evening, and she ate probably more than was wise, but while tending to her mother for the last few weeks, she'd barely been able to eat, her grief and worry too overpowering.

Lord Frostmore watched her eat with an air of amused satisfaction. "Miss Russell, permit me to ask a question." Harriet saw no harm in allowing it; she could always refuse to answer if the question was offensive to her.

She took a sip of wine. "What do you wish to ask?"

"You are not married?"

It was an unexpected question, and she gulped uncomfortably. "Married? No."

"Why not? You are a beautiful woman." The duke leaned forward in his chair to prop his elbows up on the table. Harriet knew she should be concerned with where this conversation might be going, but she felt oddly at ease with answering his question.

"I..." She paused, choosing her words carefully. "I remained with my mother when my father died. I was but fourteen when my mother remarried. The man... my stepfather...did not allow us much time to be out in society. I didn't have a chance for love." She knew it must sound ridiculous to a man like him, to speak of love and other such romantic notions, but she'd often wondered what her life would have been like if she'd met a young man in Faversham and married. Would she now be hosting a gathering to celebrate the arrival of a babe? What might her life have been like?

He set his fork down on his plate of venison and studied her. "And now? Do you consider yourself interested in love?"

"I believe so. If the right gentleman comes along, a man with honor." She wanted to marry someone like her father. A good man, a man with laughing eyes and a warm smile and a heart full of love.

"A man of honor? There is no such thing. We are all scoundrels and demons—some are merely better at hiding our horns than others." Lord Frostmore smiled wryly, his fingers toying with his still full glass of wine.

Harriet did not say anything; though she was tempted to point out that he seemed not to care that she could see his horns, and even his tail and pitchfork.

"The man doesn't have to be a saint," she added, quietly thinking it over. "But I could never marry a man who seeks to check my character at every turn like some willful pet. Despite the current laws of England, I am not property and would never marry a man who treated me as such." She hadn't given much thought to love and romance since her father died, however. She'd been living under George's shadow for so long that she'd locked that part of her dreams away.

But now, as she was thinking about it, she knew deep in her heart that she could not agree to marry a man unless he kindled some fire in her blood. She believed herself to be a woman of wild passions, and she needed a husband who would embrace that, not condemn her for it. It would not do to stifle her unpredictable nature by marriage to a man who would ruin her vivacity.

Harriet reached for her wineglass to take another drink, but her movements seemed slower than before, as though her strength was finally failing her after the ordeal of the night.

"Not all men treat their wives as property. Some men dare to love and to dream, even when it costs them their very souls." The duke pushed his chair back from the table and got to his feet and began to walk toward her.

Concerned by his slow, predatory progress in her direction, Harriet reached for her sword. Her fingers curled around the smooth metal of the handle, and she felt safe again.

"Please do not come any closer, Your Grace. I do not... I do not trust you." She pushed her chair back and stood up, but her head reeled with an unforeseen bout of dizziness, and words became suddenly harder to form.

Her sword arm wavered, the blade tip falling a few inches. She blinked; her vision doubled and swirled slowly. Harriet fell against the table for support, nearly dropping her foil since she had but one good strong arm to brace her weight with. As Lord Frostmore reached her, he attempted to gently wrest the blade from her, but she whipped it up in an arc at him. But her action was too slow, and he caught her wrist and squeezed lightly.

"Drop it," he ordered. The sword clattered to the floor. Harriet swung her free fist at his face, then screamed in pain as her shoulder twinged violently.

"You little fool," he muttered. "I didn't want you to hurt yourself." His voice was soft and gentle, and for a second she wondered if he cared about her, but how could he care? He was a devil.

Lord Frostmore caught her in his arms, and the pain lessened as whatever was happening to her deepened even further. It was as though some sorcerer had cast a powerful sleeping spell upon her. Would she wake in some distant tower, cobwebs covering her form as she woke to a kiss from a prince? Her mother used to read her fairy tales as a child, and now...now it was all she could think about. Princes... dark towers and enchantments...endless sleep.

"How...did...you...do it?" she murmured drowsily. Lord Frostmore had done this to her, whatever it was, and she clung to her consciousness, wanting to know how.

"The wine, my dear. I never drank it. I thought for sure you'd notice." His soft laughter stirred her hair as his arms tightened about her waist.

"You are the devil," Harriet said in an angry whisper as she sagged against him, now barely able to stand.

"The worst is yet to come. Luckily, you will not remember much of this night come dawn," the duke assured her.

His arm encircling her waist was the only thing keeping her upright. They exited the dining room and entered the entry hall near the stairs. Harriet latched on to a small table by the stairs, digging her fingers into the wood. The duke tugged at her weary body, but when she refused to budge, he pressed her up against the wall, letting her feel his strength as he pressed his lips to her ear.

"Now, my dear, be reasonable. Do you wish me to

tend to you here? Or should I see to you in a more private location?" One of his hands drifted down her back and over the curve of her hips, gripping the thin pink muslin gown at her waist. Harriet struggled to understand. Was he going to...?

"No...please!"

The duke kissed her forehead, brushed his knuckles over her cheek, and then released his hold so that he could bend over and wrap an arm about her legs and back, picking her up and carrying her like a child in his arms.

Harriet's head fell back, her eyes mesmerized by the spinning ceiling and the dancing light of candles that created a flaming crown around the duke's red hair. Her eyes fell shut and did not open again until her body sank into a soft bed. She forced her eyes open, just in time to see Lord Frostmore coming toward the bed. He seemed to be a dream, like a pagan god forged of lightning and moonlight, a powerful Zeus transforming from a swan to mortal form so that he might take his pleasure from the beautiful human Leda.

Harriet tried to sit up, only to collapse back onto the bed. Then she struggled to turn over and crawl away from him, but he caught her and gently settled her back in the middle of the bed.

"Stay," he commanded, then left the room.

Harriet closed her eyes, her lids simply too heavy to stay up any longer. She surrendered to whatever he had mixed into her wine. As she slipped into the darkness swallowing her up, she vowed that she would kill him if she survived the night.

❧ 4 ❧

Redmond stared at the wisp of a woman lying in his bed, trying to stop himself from feeling the guilt of his actions. She had been badly hurt—she still was—and it was made abundantly clear by the tip of her rapier that she did not trust him at all, and he couldn't blame her, given how he'd behaved. He also feared that she may have been a bit mad with panic. Surely only a woman half out of her mind and desperate would enter into his den, given what was said about him.

He'd not wanted to drug her, but as the evening wore on and her distrust showed no sign of easing, he'd had the cook slip laudanum into the wine. No doubt when she woke, she would be furious and vindicated in her distrust of him, but at least she would be well rested, and her arm would be cleaned and healing.

He had grown used to acting like a wicked man, threatening ravishment of more than one young lady foolish enough to come to his door. Not that he would have done it, but sometimes it took quite a lot to scare a marriage-minded woman away. But this one? She'd had a fear unlike the others in her eyes, as though she'd felt the fear of a man forcibly taking her before. It had shocked Redmond, and he had changed tactics, allowing her to take a sword in defense, only to have her best him like a master fencer. He'd been confused at first by her obvious skill with a blade and wondered what made her so desperate to draw upon it first in defense. He hated to think a woman like her, with such wit and bravery, would have faced something terrible like that.

So, Edward Russell's daughter was in his bed... He shook his head and moved for the door, resolved to think on the mystery of how she'd ended up here later when he had a chance to talk to her after she woke up.

Redmond met his butler in the hall. "Ah, Grindle. Did you find Miss Russell's coach?"

Grindle's face was lined with weariness, and he scrubbed a hand through his hair as he faced Redmond.

"I did, Your Grace. The grooms brought the horses and the driver back. It was as she told me. The coach was overturned and the driver badly injured. A broken leg, as far as I can tell."

"Summon the doctor. They may remain here as long as needed. I give you permission to see to the driver's needs. And Miss Russell must also be seen to when the doctor arrives. Have him set the man's leg first and then come directly to my chambers."

Grindle nodded, weariness etched in his features. "Yes, of course, Your Grace."

"One last thing, Grindle."

His butler waited expectantly.

"You and the rest of the staff are to go to bed once this is all settled. No need to rise early on the morrow. Sleep a few hours extra. You all must be half-dead from tonight's events."

Grindle's shoulders relaxed, and he offered his master a genuine smile. "Thank you, Your Grace. We would appreciate it."

The butler headed back downstairs, and Redmond paced the corridor, his boots hushing against expensive oriental carpets as he debated how best to proceed.

When he could put it off no longer, he returned to his bedchamber and sat on the edge of his bed to examine the girl again. The laudanum and alcohol had worked its magic, and she was fast asleep, no pain marring her lovely features. She was not what one would call a classic beauty, but he found her pleasing to look at, the soft curve of her cheek, her dark-gold lashes and wet blonde hair that looked like liquid ropes of burnished gold where it clung to her face and shoulders. He reached out with a trembling hand to touch her forehead. She was still damp and slightly cold. He scowled at the wet clothes she wore. The girl needed to be put into something much warmer, but it was not his place to do so. He knew he was tempting himself by putting her in his chamber, but he couldn't seem to accept the idea of sending her away to one of the dozens of other rooms. It felt...wrong.

Redmond pulled the bell cord. When his valet, Timothy, arrived, he sent him to fetch one of the upstairs maids.

Maisie, a sprightly Scottish lass recently hired on as an upstairs maid, arrived a few minutes later. "You sent for me, Your Grace?" She was hesitant in the way that a maid would be when summoned to the master's chambers after midnight, especially given his reputation. But his staff had nothing to fear.

"Rest easy, Maisie. I have need of your assistance. This way." He led her into the bedchamber and pointed at Harriet. "This is my guest, Miss Russell.

We need to get her out of her wet clothes. The doctor has been sent for, but until he arrives, we need her dry and warm. Do we have any of my late wife's nightgowns?"

"Aye, we do, Your Grace."

"Good. Fetch one at once."

Maisie bustled off to hunt down a nightgown, while Redmond carefully began to undress Harriet, starting with her boots. Her feet were small, dainty, and as he unlaced the boots he marveled at her form. She was slender, as he had noticed, but she wasn't without curves. A pretty form, even when she wasn't threatening to cut his throat. Redmond couldn't resist a smile as he set her boots down and began to roll down her stockings. He was glad she was not awake and in a position to claw his eyes out. He draped the stockings over the nearest chair by the fire to dry them out.

Maisie returned, and between them they were able to remove the simple muslin gown, and then he turned his back as Maisie removed the stays as she finished undressing Harriet and helping her into the diaphanous nightgown.

"She's all warm and dry now," Maisie announced with satisfaction, and Redmond turned around to see her.

He expected to feel unsettled by seeing another

woman wearing a nightgown he had bought for Millicent, but in truth he felt...nothing. At least nothing that turned his heart to stone. Rather, he was strangely content. Yes, *that* was the word. In the last seven years since Millicent had passed, he'd felt discontented. The empty castle, the sense of something left undone, or perhaps left behind, constantly nagging at the back of his mind. But as he looked at the little hellion in his bed, he felt strangely at ease.

"May I do anything else, Your Grace?"

"No, not tonight. Thank you, Maisie." He waited for the maid to leave before he pulled back the covers of his bed, and then with a tenderness that surprised even himself, he tucked Harriet beneath the covers and then sat down by the fire to wait for the doctor.

It was nearly an hour before there was a knock at his door. Grindle had brought the doctor to him.

"Your Grace, this is Dr. Axel."

The doctor was a young man with a great intelligence in his eyes that came with being intimately familiar with illness and death. "Your Grace."

"Thank you for coming, Doctor. As I'm sure Mr. Grindle informed you, we are taking in a pair of travelers from the storm."

"Yes, I've just seen to the driver of the coach. It was a clean break, and his leg was easy to set."

"I'm glad to hear that."

The doctor's eyes strayed to the bed and his brows rose, but he made no comment other than "Now, what ails the young lady?"

"I'm not entirely sure. She's bleeding a bit from a small wound on her head, and she's favoring her right shoulder. I gave her laudanum to relax her. She's unconscious at the moment."

Dr. Axel set his black leather satchel on the foot of the bed and pulled back the covers. He pressed his head to Harriet's chest and closed his eyes.

"Heartbeat is steady," he murmured to himself. Then he looked at Redmond and Grindle. "I need to examine her shoulder. Her gown must be pulled down a little."

Redmond joined the doctor and unfastened the silk ribbons at the throat of the gown, his hands trembling. Then he stepped back and looked to the doctor rather than Harriet as the doctor bared her right shoulder.

"Ah... 'Tis dislocated. But I can reset it." He lifted Harriet's arm in a series of slow motions and then swiftly popped it back into place. The sound made Redmond's stomach lurch. He was now thankful for having drugged the poor woman. Then Dr. Axel fixed her nightgown and examined her forehead, where he applied salve to a cut.

"She should have this." He passed Redmond a

small blue glass jar. "At least once a day on the cut. The shoulder will need looking after. Should be tender. Use more laudanum if she continues to have pain, but small doses and only when absolutely necessary. No need to create a habit with it."

"Understood." Redmond accepted the salve and took an extra bottle of laudanum when the doctor offered it to him.

"If she or the driver should worsen, don't hesitate to summon me."

"Thank you, Doctor. Grindle will see you out."

Redmond turned his focus back on Harriet once he was alone with her. She stirred briefly and murmured broken fragments of sentences that tore at his heart. What had she suffered that had left her all alone and frightened of a man's touch? A woman her age who was unmarried shouldn't have been without a chaperone. Something terrible had happened to her, and he would find out what it was.

"Who are you, Harriet? What frightens you?" He reached out to touch her face and paused. After a moment of indecision, he brushed his knuckles over her pale cheek, then settled in his chair by the fire to wait out the long night with only the shadows for company.

❅

"*HARRIET...*" A WOMAN'S VOICE PULLED AT HARRIET in the quiet darkness of deep sleep, drawing her into a waking dream. Harriet stirred in the large bed, puzzled by the strangeness of it. It was not her bed, not the one she'd slept in at Thursley Manor for the last six years. That bed had been a small piece of furniture with sensible linens and a pale-blue faded coverlet. This was a tall four-poster bed with dark wood and red damask curtains. It was a bed of beauty, of seduction, even. How had she come to be here?

Firelight from a hearth across the room cast shadows on the bedchamber, illuminating the figure lying back in one of the chairs. The man was asleep, his long, muscular legs stretched out and one arm limp over the armrest.

"*Harriet...,*" the feminine voice called again, and the crackling of the fire seem to slow down. A sliver of moonlight detached itself from the thick milky beams pouring in from the windows.

Harriet blinked, awestruck as the moonbeam seemed to gather within itself like shimmering stardust as it became something she recognized. A willowy female form.

"*Harriet...*" The syllables of her name were dragged out in a fervent murmur as the figure raised a hand and pointed to the man asleep in the chair. Her face was so melancholy, so full of sorrow, that Harriet's throat closed up and she choked down a sob.

"Wait," she whispered, but the phantom was already drifting away, melting into a tapestry of a pair of stags in the woods.

Blinking again, Harriet noticed the crackling fire was back to normal and the rain was plinking against the windows. She sank back against the pillows of the bed. Her mind, so clear just moments ago, was now fighting sleep again. As she closed her eyes and burrowed deep into the blankets and inhaled the dark, masculine scent of the sheets, she swore she heard one last distant call.

"Harriet..."

REDMOND JERKED AWAKE IN HIS CHAIR AT THE sound of a soft cry. He leaned forward and saw that Harriet was twisted in his bed, her face lit by the dusky light of the fire. Tears coated her cheeks, making her skin shine.

"Miss Russell." He had assumed she was awake, but she did not respond to him. He rose from his chair and tossed another log onto the fire before he came over to the bed. She was tangled up in the bedclothes, her body's position clearly uncomfortable.

"Wait... Don't go..." Harriet's murmur was so full of loss and pain, he wondered who she was dreaming about.

He wiped the tears from her face with a handkerchief, stunned by his desire to be gentle with the stranger who had trespassed in his domain. Ever since Millicent and Thomas had died, he had demanded solitude, a quiet house to himself so he could bury himself in regret and guilt. It was no less than he deserved.

Suddenly the hairs on his neck rose, and he felt the faintest caress of something over his skin, like cool fingertips. He sensed it, sensed the presence that often came to haunt him just after midnight. His grandmother would have called it the hour of the wolf, where the sleepless were haunted by their deepest fears, when ghosts and demons were at their most powerful. He looked around as he always did but saw nothing.

"She doesn't belong here, not with me." He spoke softly to the room, not sure why he needed to speak at all, or what otherworldly thing might be lingering in the shadows.

Harriet grasped his hand, which had brushed against her cheek.

"Please don't leave," she murmured, her eyes still closed. "Please... I'm so cold."

Redmond gasped as he tripped and fell onto the bed. He would have sworn it felt as if someone had just pushed him. But it was madness to think such a thing, wasn't it?

Harriet burrowed closer to him, and before Redmond could extricate himself, he found himself holding Harriet. He could have done anything he liked to her, she was that helpless, still under the hypnotic sway of the laudanum. But he was not a monster, not the monster he pretended to be, at any rate. Whatever cruelty she had endured elsewhere, he would not perpetuate any on her here.

He pulled the coverlet up again around their bodies, not caring that he was still fully clothed. He had slept many a night in worse conditions in the last seven years, and perhaps it would help assure her that he had not taken advantage of her vulnerable state if she should regain her senses too soon. He closed his eyes, wondering how Edward Russell's daughter had ended up here in his arms.

Redmond had been one of Russell's students more than a decade ago, just after he left Cambridge. He had felt a bond to the fencing master, like he would have to an older brother. The man had been honorable, amusing, and openhearted. To hear of his death tonight had shocked Redmond, but he had been so angry at having a young woman here disturbing him that he hadn't processed the fact that Edward Russell was dead.

And now here he was, holding the man's daughter, a daughter who was lonely and tempting. She was also the same tender age as his late wife. Pain seized his heart, and he squeezed his eyes even tighter, hoping he would sleep soon because he was not going to cry about the past.

Not again.

GEORGE HALIFAX SMILED SMUGLY AS HE LEFT THE bedside of his wife, who now lay cold and lifeless. He'd slept late after dinner, and by the time he'd returned to Emmeline's bed, she'd finally drawn her last breath. It'd taken her long enough to die. Now he was clear to get what he wanted, what he had craved for so many years. He walked down to the room his men had taken Harriet into, and his grin widened at the sight of the locked door. She was inside, waiting for him, waiting to ease his needs. If she resisted, as he expected her to, he would call for his men to assist him in subduing her. She'd always been such a willful creature, no doubt because she had wasted her time learning the art of fencing when she should have been practicing needlepoint or some other frivolous activity. But it had made for a fiery creature he would delight in bedding and breaking until he molded her into what he desired.

He pulled the heavy brass key from his pocket and inserted it into the keyhole. He opened the door, his heart pounding with excitement, anticipating the chase. He waited for his caged pet to fly at him in a rage, but there was no movement in the dark room.

"Harriet?" he murmured. "Your dear mother has passed, and your father has come to comfort you."

More silence. He stepped into the room and retrieved a lamp, lighting it with a pair of strikers he found on the side table. He waved the lamp around the room, casting its light over every corner as a black rage built up inside him. The room was empty. The window was open, with a trail of bedsheets knotted together dropping down to the gardens one floor below. His pretty little bird had flown away. When he caught up with her, she would regret ever escaping him.

5

When Harriet woke, warm sunlight illuminated the lavish bedchamber she was in. She blinked in confusion, expecting to see watery pale sunlight fogging up the glass windows of a room in Thursley Manor, yet she found herself in the same room she'd dreamt about.

Not a dream...

She shifted in the bed and groaned as every muscle protested. She winced and put a hand to her head as memories from the night before trickled back.

She had fled Thursley while her mother lay dying. The coach had overturned during a terrible storm. She had fought the Devil of Dover with a fencing foil...and won? Yes, but then the memories grew fuzzier, like thick wool blanketing a window she desperately wished to see through. She remembered dinner, and her shoulder in pain, and then... She gasped.

Lord Frostmore had drugged her, and now she was in a bedroom. She lifted the blankets and found she was wearing a nightgown of fine quality. She had never touched something like this before, let alone worn one. With trembling hands, she pulled her gown up but saw no bruises, no blood on her thighs. Had he not taken his pleasure, then, while she lay helpless?

The bedchamber door opened, and a lovely young woman with dark hair and light-brown eyes entered. She was humming to herself but paused when she saw that Harriet was awake. She glanced down at the tray she was holding and lifted it up slightly as she looked at Harriet.

"Good morning, miss, my name is Maisie. I'm to tend to you as a lady's maid while you're staying here. His Grace thought you might be hungry. May I come in?"

Harriet nodded mutely, and the girl came in to place the tray on the bed. Toast, a jar of marmalade, a hard-boiled egg, and some peaches were all set on a pale-blue-and-white pattern set of china. A tiny vase of chrysanthemums filled the air with their sweet floral perfume. The duke must have a hothouse on his grounds somewhere. It was far too cold for anything to grow outside this time of year.

"Tea or coffee?" the maid asked.

"Er... tea, thank you."

"A bit of orange pekoe, all right?" Maisie's lilting Scottish accent was bright and cheery. It managed to put Harriet at ease a little.

"Orange pekoe? I've never heard of it."

"It's from Denmark."

"Does it taste like oranges?" Harriet asked as the maid began to prepare a cup.

"His Grace says it's not a flavor, but a reference to the noble house of Orange-Nassau, who brought the tea to Europe a hundred years ago. He says the pekoe is the top bud of the tea plant." The maid handed her a hot cup of tea, and the scent was divine.

"And how did you come to learn so much about it?"

Maisie chuckled. "I often pester His Grace, when he's in a mood to talk. He knows quite a bit about a lot of things. He's traveled all over the continent, even as far as Bavaria."

"Oh?" Harriet found herself wanting to know more about him, but she was afraid of him, and the fact that she couldn't remember fully what had happened the night before between them only strengthened those concerns.

"He's..." The maid paused as she retrieved Harriet's muddy muslin dress off the floor. "Well, he's quite gentle and scholarly, when he's not in a black mood." Maisie eyed the clothes in her arms thoughtfully. "Oh, dear. You cannot wear these again. Too torn up to repair, not with my poor sewing skills. I'll see what I can find for you."

"Oh, please, I don't want to be any trouble, and I really must leave, at any rate. Did Mr. Grindle find my coach driver, Mr. Johnson? He was injured when I came here last night."

"Oh, aye. A pair of our grooms found him. Mr. Johnson's leg is broken, but Dr. Axel set it, and your man is resting in the servants' quarters. The groom who found him happened to say you had no luggage?" Maisie asked.

"I didn't." Harriet lay back against the pillows, feeling suddenly very tired again.

"Never you mind then, miss. Like I said, I'll find something for you to wear. Now eat up and sleep." The maid turned to leave.

"But—"

Maisie halted and looked over her shoulder. "Yes, miss?"

"The duke... Did he...?" She blushed and stared down at the bedclothes she clutched hard enough that her knuckles were white.

"Did he what, miss?" Maisie inquired, her tone softer now.

"I don't remember much after dinner. He gave me something... Laudanum, I think."

"Aye, he did. Your shoulder was badly out of joint, and His Grace said you were close to hysterics. He had the cook put a bit of it in the wine and carried you up here. The doctor set your shoulder and tended to your cuts. I changed your clothes myself." Maisie gave her a meaningful look of reassurance.

"Then he didn't...?" She still couldn't voice her fears.

"No, miss. That's not his way. He's..." Maisie hesitated.

"He's what?"

"It's no' for me to say, miss."

"Please tell me. Surely you know of his reputation."

"Well that's the thing, miss. He's more bark than bite. He was hurt once, a long time ago, and he does not let anyone get too close anymore. But he's a good man, once you get him to trust you. At least, that's been my experience."

Harriet watched the maid collect her wet stockings from over the back of a chair, her pensive expression brightening a little as she faced Harriet again.

"Ring the bell cord by the bed if you need anything. I'll be back with clothes once I find something that will suit you."

"Thank you, Maisie."

"You're welcome, miss."

After the maid had gone, Harriet's appetite returned, and she ate her breakfast and had two cups of the orange pekoe tea. Then she lay back in the bed, half-asleep, and focused on the sunlight creeping across the room.

Her gaze fell upon the radiantly colored tapestries of the woods and the stags within them. Had she really dreamt of a lustrous silver figure stealing into them, then evaporating like an errant pool of mist? She remembered quite clearly the figure raising a hand to point at a man asleep in the chair by the fire. It had to be the duke, and the scorching flames had illuminated his masculine form into a black, haunting silhouette that stole her breath. Had she really been visited by a spirit last night? If she had, what did it want? What was it trying to tell her by pointing at the duke as he slept?

Exhaustion tugged at her limbs, pulling her back down into the bed again, but her fear and unease from the night before was fading quickly, and she no longer feared falling asleep.

Harriet carefully lay upon her left side and closed

her eyes. When she woke, it must have been a number of hours later. A haze of dappled sunlight lit the wooded tapestries as though it were a real forest where the stags might have raised their long, elegant limbs with ease, stepping clean out of the threaded world sewn around them. The magic of the room— with the added scent of someone, most likely the duke—lingered strongly here. Had he come to see her while she slept? The idea unnerved her, but there was very little fear left at the thought. Maisie was right, he was like that intimidating black dog of his, Devil. All bark and no bite.

She sat up, pushed the covers away, and slipped out of bed. The stones beneath her feet were cool, but not cold as she expected. Harriet went to the fireplace and added a few logs, despite the fact that her shoulder still ached, but the pain was far more manageable. She studied the cut upon her brow in a mirror and washed her face in the white porcelain basin. The cold water felt good and woke her up a bit. Weariness still tugged at her limbs, but she was content to keep moving, stretching her legs and regaining some of her mobility. Maisie returned to find her practicing some fencing positions, ones she could execute without requiring her right arm.

"Miss?" Maisie tilted her head. "Are you well? I'm not certain you should be out of bed."

"Yes, I'm quite well. I needed to move or else I'd become stiff." Harriet returned to the bed. Maisie carried over a large white box and set it before her.

"I found this up in the attic. Been stored there and was never worn, as far as I know." She opened the box and pulled out a beautiful gown.

"Oh... It's lovely. I couldn't possibly wear it," Harriet protested.

"Nonsense. You will look fetching in it, miss. I've dried your stays and have a clean chemise ready for you."

Maisie helped to remove her nightgown, and she was dressed in fresh undergarments before Maisie helped her don the dress. It was made of green silk, and it had an open robe with a matching underskirt of white silk. It was what her mother would have called a 'greatcoat' dress.

The turned-down collar with patterned lapels gave the appearance of a man's military coat, yet there was a feminine elegance to it. Harriet glanced down at the outer skirts and saw the ends of the side panels had been stitched back, which gave the illusion of additional panels in the same slightly masculine fashion, as though she were wearing a full-length military coat. But there was nothing masculine about the dress. The bright-green and cream silk called to mind the colors of summer lawns and clouds. Tiny pink flowers were embroidered along the hem and the bodice, making it look as though Harriet had rushed into a field of wildflowers and rolled about until her gown was covered with them.

Maisie brushed her palms over her skirts and nodded to herself in approval. "Very fetching."

"I still think I shouldn't wear this." Whoever had owned this dress deserved it more than she did.

"We have a mountain of clothes that are still boxed and unworn. The duchess—"

"These are the *duchess's* clothes?" Harriet tried to remove the dress. Maisie pushed her hands away.

"His Grace had them ordered as a wedding present, but she didn't much care for them."

"But... They're so lovely." Harriet felt like a queen in the gown.

"Yes, they are. Her Grace simply had different tastes. You are nearly the same size as her in the bust and hips, though she was a little taller. I can tailor the unworn gowns if you like. I have skill enough for that."

Harriet bit her lip and looked at herself in the looking glass. "It won't upset him to see me in these?"

"I dinna think so," Maisie admitted honestly. "He ordered the gowns, but when she chose her own instead, he was sad. It may do him good to see these worn by a lovely woman." Maisie's gaze had moved to her hair. "Shall I style it better for you?"

"Oh, could you? I haven't had it done in ages. I wasn't allowed to have a maid at Thursley."

Maisie's eyes widened. "Thursley? That's in Faversham, isn't it?"

"Yes, but please don't speak of it to anyone. I must insist."

The maid's expression turned thoughtful, and she bit her lip. "Are you in some trouble, miss? I'm sure His Grace would protect you if you were."

"That's just it—I'm quite certain he wouldn't." She took a chance to trust Maisie. "My father died when I was young, and my mother married a terrible man. That man is hunting me now, likely this very minute. He is an acquaintance of Lord Frostmore's. I don't want the duke to discover he's harboring a fugitive from someone he considers a friend. He may choose to turn me over to my stepfather."

The maid ran a brush through Harriet's hair and was silent a long moment. "What is your stepfather's name?"

"George Halifax." Harriet was almost afraid to breathe it aloud lest she summon him like some demon.

"I can say in all honesty that we haven't had anyone by that name visit here. His Grace rarely goes into town. And we are a ways from Faversham. Of course, I've only worked here a few months. Could be that I'm wrong, but is it possible your stepfather lied to you?"

Harriet wanted to believe her, but she was afraid. If she was wrong, George might catch up with her and... She shuddered and tried not to think about what he would do.

"It's possible, but I do not wish to risk it."

"Then I shall keep silent, miss."

"Thank you, Maisie." The two of them shared a smile.

"Come on. The housekeeper, Mrs. Breland, will want to show you the house. I told her I would fetch you once you were dressed."

"Mrs. Breland? I didn't meet her last night."

"Most of us were in bed when you arrived." Maisie giggled. "She gave Mr. Grindle quite the dressing down this morning for not waking her, but if you ask me, he let her sleep because he fancies her."

"Does he? Is she lovely?" Harriet asked.

"She is, but she tries to act severe. But when she thinks she's not being watched, she smiles and lights up the room."

They continued to gossip about the staff as Maisie escorted her downstairs to the great hall on the ground floor. A tall woman with auburn hair threaded with silver was busy issuing orders to a pair of foot-men. She turned at their approach and offered a polite but reserved smile.

"Miss Russell?"

Harriet nearly dropped into a curtsy at the house-keeper's regal beauty. She wore a black dress made of fine silk, and the cut was simple but elegant. "Yes, that's me."

"I am Mrs. Breland. I regret I was not able to assist you last evening when you arrived. I trust you are feeling better this morning?"

"I am, thank you. Maisie has been wonderful looking after me."

"Maisie is a good girl, though I hope she did not talk your ear off." Mrs. Breland nodded at the maid, who smiled encouragingly at Harriet before leaving her alone with the housekeeper.

"Now, I will take you on a quick tour of the house so you won't lose your way. At night the corridors can feel much the same, and it can be very easy to get lost."

For the next hour, Harriet followed Mrs. Breland and became acquainted with the rambling old manor house with its progression of stately rooms. There was a great hall, which had once been the toast of kings, at least according to the housekeeper. Now it was a room full of marble busts and sculptures. The

timber beams along the walls had been removed
twenty years before and replaced with fluted stone
Doric columns that reflected a pure Italian Renais-
sance style.

Harriet had never seen such a grand home; it
dwarfed Thursley Manor. There seemed to be a
magic that had settled into the stones, sometimes a
dark and frightening magic in the shadows of some
rooms. But at other times, when sunlight streamed
through high windows, it painted brilliant colors
upon walls covered with damask silk wallpaper or
intricately woven tapestries, creating a light, joyful
enchantment. In those moments, she felt love
burning clear through her, almost overwhelmingly so.
This house had seen much over the centuries. Heart-
break and blinding love in equal measure.

Harriet's heart swelled as Mrs. Breland next
ushered her into a portrait gallery. At its entrance
stood a tall suit of armor. The metal was polished to
a shine, but there was evidence of nicks and
scratches on its surface. Whoever had worn this
armor had seen battle. It had tasted the bite of a
blade. She looked at the helmet and swore she could
feel the grave gaze of a medieval ghost staring back at
her. But the armor said nothing. It was a mute, stal-
wart guardian over the gallery of portraits just
beyond.

Mrs. Breland gestured down the massive corridor. "This is the long gallery."

Filmy red curtains caught the light, so as to prevent the sun from fading the abundance of oil paintings that covered the walls. Harriet strained to see each and every piece. In the center of the room, three portraits were hung close together. There was a man in the middle, flanked by another man on the left and a woman upon the right.

"A fair likeness, I think," Mrs. Breland mused next to Harriet.

"That's the duke in the center?" She knew it was —there was no mistaking his eyes and the red flame of his hair. He stood with quiet intensity, posing for the artist without flair or pomp. Harriet's eyes drifted to the other man. He was beautiful, his features perfect in every way, and there was a glint of humor about his mouth that made him instantly likable. "Who is that?"

"That is Thomas, His Grace's younger brother. He passed seven years ago."

Harriet desperately wanted to ask how, but she dared not upset Mrs. Breland.

"And that next to them is the late Duchess of Frostmore."

Harriet focused on the pretty woman with graceful features and dark hair. A tingle of foreboding rippled like quicksilver beneath her skin. She had no doubt that this was the woman she had dreamt about.

"Mrs. Breland, how did she die?" She regretted the question the instant she spoke it.

"It was a terrible accident near the cliffs. She fell. His Grace and his brother almost perished as well."

"His Grace was present when she died?"

"He was." Mrs. Breland's brusque tone warned Harriet that she would have no more luck in obtaining answers on the subject. Mrs. Breland showed her the rest of the house, including the library. After that, the housekeeper left her on her own.

Harriet trod softly now on the carpets in the corridors as she returned to the great hall, where she found the duke engaged in a game of tug-of-war with his giant schnauzer. Devil was growling and tugging hard on a large knotted rope. Devil thrashed his head from side to side, trying to wrench the rope away from his master, but without success.

"Come on, boy. I won't let you win that easily!" The duke's laugh was deep and hearty, not the cold laugh she remembered from last night. Harriet lingered in the shadows at the top of the stairs, not wanting to intrude upon the happy scene. Finally, Lord Frostmore relinquished his hold on the rope, and Devil trotted off to another room with his prize. Harriet chose that moment to come down. Lord Frostmore's back was to her, but he spoke as she reached the last stair.

"I trust you slept well, Miss Russell?" His tone was soft, carrying a slight sensuality that made her think of beds and activities other than sleeping. She froze. She hadn't made a sound on the steps, yet he had sensed her.

"I slept tolerably well, but my head still pains me. No doubt a parting gift from the laudanum you gave me," she replied coldly as he turned to face her. He wore no coat, only buff breeches, a white shirt, and a silver waistcoat. Seeing him dressed like this, more free to move about, made her stomach flutter with nerves. For a long moment his gaze swept over her, and she wondered what he could be thinking as he saw her in his wife's old gown. But his contemplative look revealed nothing of his thoughts.

"I gave you only a little laudanum. I wouldn't wish your pain upon anyone, and you were in terrible pain."

"You could have asked me," she argued.

"You have my deepest apologies, but you wouldn't have trusted me. We battled only minutes before."

Harriet stiffened as he approached her. "Because you threatened to ravish me."

"My solitude had been disturbed, and I was angry. I would never have harmed you." He stepped closer into her space until she came level with his shoulders.

"And how was I to know that?"

He shrugged. "You couldn't have, not with my reputation and the rather theatrical weather outside to enhance your mistrust. Hence my course of action. As frightening as it seemed at the time, I assure you my intention was only to assist you." His topaz-colored eyes searched her face for something; for what she wasn't sure, but it made her feel small and feminine in a way that excited her.

She couldn't deny her attraction to him now. He lacked the finesse a London dandy might possess, nor did he have the angelic beauty of his brother. But there was a raw, untarnished purity in his looks that made him physically admirable. With his red hair and proud patrician features, he was beautiful in his own way.

He clasped his hands behind his back. "You are welcome to stay for a time. I've decided it has been good for my staff to have someone else to fuss over."

"But I can't. I must leave for Calais."

Lord Frostmore placed a palm on the banister next to her. Her heart jumped wildly, and her mouth went dry as he leaned in toward her. A strange yet exciting magnetism held her still as he peered at her.

Other than her stepfather, she'd never been the focus of a man before, and she found that she liked the duke's attention, even if it was a little frightening.

"What awaits you in Calais?"

The pit of her stomach tingled, and she couldn't help but stare at his mouth, the full lips that looked impossibly soft. "My father had family there," she whispered as his focus drifted down along the length of her body. The duke disturbed her in ways she had never imagined, yet he inspired more longing than fear in her. Such an attraction was nothing short of perilous, yet she could feel it building within her.

"Stay." He spoke the word as a mixture of a command and a plea.

"Why? We are strangers, and hostile ones at that," she reminded him.

His lips twitched. "Oh, nonsense. I greet everyone like that." He leaned in slightly, enough that the heat of his body emanated off him, warming her in the most delicious way.

"With a sword fight?" She almost smiled, damn him.

"No, that was only for you. But everyone who visits tastes my lack of charm and overall displeasure. You see, I'm a wicked man. A wicked man with wicked desires and a terrible past that is only whispered about in the shadows. But I'm sure you're familiar with the stories."

"I have heard...," she admitted.

With their faces so close, there was a brief and wild moment she thought about kissing him, thought about how it had felt last night even when she'd been afraid of him. What would it feel like to kiss him now when she wasn't?

"Tell me, what do the villagers say of me these days? The stories seem to be getting positively Gothic as of late."

His scent enveloped her as he raised her chin so their eyes locked. She could smell leather and rain. Had he been outside recently?

"They say...you killed your brother and your wife."

He blinked and dropped his hand from under her chin, looking away, his eyes suddenly distant. "Some days it feels like the truth."

"It isn't?" she asked, then immediately regretted it.

"Not in the way you probably believe." He stepped away and began to leave. Harriet stared after him, utterly baffled. She couldn't let him walk away with her questions unanswered, but neither could she pry directly. She decided to follow him at a discreet distance, to see if he would volunteer more information, but he never did. It was only when he stepped into the library that he spoke.

"Either come in or find your amusement elsewhere, Miss Russell. I'll not have you stalk me like a black cat in the shadows."

A little ruffled, she came into the library and watched him collect a few volumes of political treatises and set them on a nearby reading table, which he then sat down at. The light coming in from the windows lit his hair like flames.

"I did not take you to be an avid reader, Lord Frostmore."

He arched a brow as she settled down across from him and stole the next book in his trio of chosen volumes.

"Given the brief duration of our acquaintance, I could say the same of you." His tone was half-amused, half-frustrated. Harriet suspected he was not accustomed to conversation.

"Well, I do like to read."

"And fence," he added.

She blushed. "My father used to take me to his lessons with the young lords. I learned much. My father believed women ought to have as much physical activity as men. My mother was very healthy until..." Her breath caught in her throat, and pain tore through her. How had she so easily buried thoughts of her mother?

"What? What's the matter?" Frostmore observed in concern.

"I..." She bit her lip and closed her eyes. When she opened them, the duke had risen from his chair and came over to kneel at her side. He offered her a handkerchief. She accepted it, feeling so very silly to cry and even sillier when she glimpsed a stag's head crowned by briar roses embroidered on the cloth. His family crest, no doubt. The Devil of Dover had given her his personal handkerchief.

"When I left my home, my mother was dying. I think she must be gone now. She was already so close before...I had to leave. I managed not to think of it until now. And that makes me a wretched daughter."

Frostmore watched her, his eyes suddenly warm. He reached up and covered one of her hands with his.

"You were injured and ill. Your mother wouldn't blame you for that. Dry your eyes." She dabbed at her tears and drew in a shaky breath, then returned the handkerchief to him. He tucked it into his trouser pocket. "Tell me, why did you leave?" Frostmore leaned back on the edge of the reading table beside her. His question caught her off guard, and she was tempted to answer openly and honestly, but she still didn't trust to tell him the truth, at least not all of it.

"Do you know a man by the name of George

Halifax? He owns Thursley Manor in Faversham." She held her breath, waiting to see if her fears would be confirmed.

"Halifax?" He thought it over, then slowly shook his head. "No, I don't know the man. I spend little time in Faversham, and since my wife and brother died, I haven't been there except perhaps once or twice a year." His face held an honesty that she decided she would try to trust. If he was lying, she was doomed, but if he wasn't...she might find an ally.

"My mother remarried after my father died. But the man she chose was vile. That man is George Halifax. While she was healthy she kept him away from me, but when she fell ill he saw his chance, and my mother told me to flee. So I did. I left her alone with him..." She feared deep down that George may have hastened her mother's death.

She wasn't sure what she expected Lord Frostmore to say, but he simply picked up the book she'd been about to peruse and handed it to her.

"You did as your mother wished. You did not fail her." Then he sat down and opened his book again. After a long moment, he spoke. "And I do like to read. It is one of the few pleasures I allow myself to indulge in."

She'd never been one to be overly open, and it

seemed Lord Frostmore was the same, yet she didn't feel lonely sitting here with him. He knew she was in pain, both of the body and the spirit. He'd offered comfort and kind words, but he hadn't pushed her to speak of it again. It was a relief not to be pressed about it.

They both read in silence until the shadows stretched across the library.

"You truly wish for me to stay here?" she asked.

Frostmore raised his eyes from the page. "I do. Christmas will be here soon, and the Channel will be full of icebergs. You don't want to make the voyage, even one so short, in poor weather. Wait until spring."

"But I only have enough money to pay for my voyage and a few days beyond. I must find work in order to pay for lodgings and food."

The duke steepled his fingers, looking at her in silent contemplation. "Stay here until spring. You need not pay me anything."

"Your Grace, I cannot—"

"Oh, what are you concerned about? Scandal? Who would care? No one comes on my lands. No one would know you are here. Consider my home a private refuge until you are ready to voyage in the spring."

"May I have some time to think upon it?" she

asked. He answered with a nod and then stood and left the room. This time she didn't follow him.

How strange that she would find refuge with a man whom so many others feared. Perhaps he was less of a devil than they believed—at least, that's what she hoped.

6

Redmond strode out the front of Frostmore and whistled sharply. Devil bounded into view and joined him outside as a groom brought his horse forward. The white Arabian mare, Winter's Frost, was his favorite. Many men favored stallions or geldings, but not Redmond. He had purchased her after burying his wife and brother, and her gentle spirit and exceptional speed were a balm to his soul. He rode her for miles, especially when the weather was fair, and it helped him feel like he was escaping his sorrows, if only for a little while.

As he mounted her and rode out across the lands of his home, he watched the fall leaves turn from gold to brittle brown, a sure sign that winter was on the way. The promise of snow was carried upon the wind, its bite bringing Redmond's thoughts more clearly into focus. Had he really asked Harriet to stay through the spring?

In truth, he admitted he wanted her to. She was rash, bold, and uncompromising, but she wasn't like the other women who had come to him. The ones who came to tempt him into offering marriage. Marriage was far from Harriet's thoughts. It was her mother she was grieving for, a loss deep enough that it rattled the cage he had placed around his own heart.

Her tears today had tugged at him, beckoning him closer to her. Perhaps because her grief was genuine, as his own had been seven years ago. To lose a wife and brother had emptied his heart of feelings and left him in a dark, cold abyss. Seeing Harriet face that same dark pain as she realized her mother was likely gone, and that she'd not been there to help her...

He felt a sudden chill inside. How long had it been since he'd felt something, *truly* felt something? All it had taken was a hellion to attack him with a blade and then weep over her mother's death, and all of his own pain, which he'd thought long buried, had come flooding back.

A desperate desire to see the cliffs drove him in

their direction. When he finally pulled back on his mare's reins, he was but twenty feet away from the edge where he had tried to end his own life seven years ago. He always rode this close—the cliffs called to him, asking him to take the leap he had promised back then. But he didn't dismount, didn't do anything but stare out at the wintry sea beyond the edge.

Heavy clouds rolled in, and whitecaps topped the waves. The pull toward the edge faded. Instead, he felt an invisible thread tied to Frostmore Hall, and a glimmer of hope seemed to fill it with a pulsing energy, like a guiding light on the shore. Devil barked suddenly and began to jump, though there was nothing around to be seen. Redmond's mare danced back and forth uneasily.

"Quiet, Devil," Redmond commanded.

The dog barked at thin air for a few seconds longer and then stopped. Just then, Redmond swore he saw something out of the corner of his eye. Something that made no sense, something that wasn't *possible*. He had seen Thomas. And just as quickly, that sense of someone being there on the cliffs with him was gone. Devil became docile again, and the horse steadied herself.

Redmond dug his heels into her flanks and rode back to the manor house. The turreted structure stood proud beneath the overcast skies as sunlight surrendered to the approaching winter storm. The gates stood open, and he raced past them to the front door. A groom met him to collect the horse's reins. Devil darted up ahead of Redmond and into the house.

As Redmond jogged up the stone steps and entered his home, a flash of soft crème and green caught his eye. He froze as he watched her stunning gown illuminate her gold hair and paint her like a nymph who had escaped the woods she had been born into.

He'd once believed Millicent should have worn that dress, but now he was glad she never had. He could imagine no other woman but Harriet would do it justice. He wanted to run up the stairs, catch her waist, and bury his face in her neck, covering her throat with kisses before he stole her lips and...

What is happening to me? He was losing his mind, that was what. His attraction to this woman was overpowering. Perhaps he'd simply been alone for too long? Or maybe it was something more, something that scared him because he couldn't open his heart again.

"Your Grace." She came toward him with tentative steps, the slight train of her gown whispering over the stones of the hall.

"Miss Russell." He gazed upon her with longing.

"I would like to stay through the spring, if you still wish to extend the invitation." She drew her bottom lip between her teeth in a show of nerves, and he was powerless to resist her. She could have demanded a thousand stars and he would have tried to give them to her.

"Yes, that would be very good. I'll have Grindle ask the cook to serve supper in an hour, if you wish?"

"Thank you." She paused. "I should speak to Mrs. Breland about moving to a new bedchamber. I am feeling better, and you should have your chambers returned to you." Her cheeks blossomed with a tender blush that quickened his heart. There was an innocence to her, one that he suspected would always remain within her. Yet she wasn't naïve or silly like others he had met. She had seen pain, felt loss, had her heart hurt by both, yet she hadn't given over to anger, hate, or cloying despair as he had. Redmond envied her that strength of character.

"Very well. Tell Mrs. Breland I recommend the Pearl Room."

Something akin to hope flashed in Harriet's eyes. "Would you show me the way? I believe Mrs. Breland is speaking to the kitchen staff right now, and I would hate to disturb her. If you don't mind, that is."

Strangely, he didn't. His instincts should have

been to run from her and from this entire situation, but instead he nodded and held out his arm to her. She tucked her arm in his, and they ascended the stairs together. He remembered escorting Millicent up like this, both of them still in their wedding clothes. He had been so elated, so overjoyed to have a wife, to have someone to belong to him. Yet there had been a tightness around Millicent's eyes and a hint of worry that had darkened her brow. He'd mistaken it for a bride's wedding nerves. How foolish he'd been not to see her anxiety for what it was, not to see that she loved his brother.

"What's the matter, Your Grace?" Harriet's question forced him out of his thoughts. He looked down at her, frowning slightly.

"I beg your pardon. I was lost in thought." He was not about to admit that he was thinking of another woman, or the mistakes he had made.

"Oh..." He could sense the disappointment in her tone.

"I'm sorry, Miss Russell. It's just been a long time since I was in a position to entertain company, and it seems I'm out of practice."

"Yes, of course," she replied, and her lips hinted at a smile. "That does happen when one routinely chases away one's visitors."

Redmond found his chuckle had become rusty from disuse. "Yes, I suppose you're right."

They went up the curving staircase until they were one floor above his bedchamber. He stopped in front of an ornately carved door and opened it for her.

"This is the Pearl Room." He waited for her to enter ahead of him.

"Why is it called that?" Harriet asked.

Redmond followed her inside, admiring her figure from behind. "See for yourself."

She pulled her arm free of his to go and explore the room. A tall four-poster bed was decorated with curtains of black velvet embroidered with silver and gold. Pearls were sewn into the curtains, creating patterns like falling rain amid the embroidered silver and gold stars.

"It's a shower of stardust," he said, reaching out to touch the curtains. "That's what my grandmother used to call it."

Harriet's eyes were wide with awe as her hands joined his to brush over the velvet.

"It's the most beautiful thing I've ever seen. No, I cannot stay here. This room is more suited to a..." Her voice trailed off.

"A duchess? Yes. It is. Please, stay. A room like this should not remain empty."

Her blush vanished as she suddenly paled. "Did your wife stay here?"

"Millicent? No, she stayed in the Green Velvet Room, or my bed when I..." He swallowed hard as shame colored his tone.

"When you what?" Harriet looked up at him with an innocence that made him want to hold her close in a way he'd never expected.

"When I asked her to. She was not fond of sharing my bed." He wasn't sure why he admitted to such an intimate detail of his life, but he didn't want her to think he and Millicent had had a perfect marriage. He wanted... What did he want? For this woman he barely knew to see how empty his life had been of love? To pity him?

To love him?

"You have a lovely bedchamber, Your Grace. Forgive me for saying so, but I don't think the duchess should have slept apart from you."

"You don't believe in separate rooms?" That intrigued him. Most of society expected separate rooms.

"No, I don't. When it's a love match, I believe a man and woman who love one another should share a bed. Perhaps my view is affected by my childhood perception. My parents were not aristocrats, and our home in the Cotswolds was small by comparison. My parents shared a bedchamber, and I believe it kept them in love, to be so near to one another."

Redmond touched a pearl on the nearest curtain. He'd longed for a love match and had foolishly thought Millicent was his.

"I agree. The intimacy of sleeping beside another person is remarkable. Few barriers exist between two people who choose to share a bed, to share dreams and midnight whispers." He thought of how Harriet had slept in his bed last night and how he had wished to hold her, to sleep beside her. How could he long for that in a way that seemed so much deeper than it had ever been with Millicent?

Because Millicent had never truly been his. She'd belonged to Thomas from the moment they had met. But Harriet? She was someone who might yet belong to him and he to her. The thought surprised him, but he did not deny it. After seven years, he wished to shed his solitude, yet he was still afraid to trust in love again. And so was she.

"I shall light a few of the lamps for you. Please, make yourself comfortable. Maisie will continue to see to your needs for as long as you stay. I'll have a footman come up shortly to light the fire."

He caught her hand and bowed over it, kissing

her fingertips. She didn't pull her hand away, which at least reassured him that she no longer feared him in any way. He left her alone and carried that little bit of hope with him back down the spiral stairs.

HARRIET SPUN AROUND IN THE PEARL ROOM LONG after Redmond had gone. She felt giddy and excited staying in such a stately, dreamy room. The brooding duke she had feared was fading like a mirage before her eyes. She no longer saw him as a devil, but as a lost soul. A man still lost and still in pain.

She wished she knew the truth of what had happened to his wife and brother. That was the only mystery that still worried her. But perhaps she would soon coax that story out of him. She also admitted that she could not envision this man as being friends or even acquaintances with her stepfather now that she was coming to know him. When she'd first arrived last night, she'd refused to trust him, but now? She felt it might be possible.

Maisie knocked on the door a few minutes later and entered with a stack of boxes in her arms. Timothy the valet followed behind, carrying a set of even larger boxes.

"We emptied the attic, with His Grace's

approval," she said as she put the boxes on the bed. Timothy added his load to the pile, and with a wink at Maisie, he left the two of them alone.

"A bit of a rogue, that one is." The maid giggled as she eyed the valet's retreating form.

"Who? Timothy?" Harriet asked as she helped Maisie open a few of the larger dress boxes.

"Aye. He's courting me. We only got permission from Mrs. Breland yesterday. Normally that sort of thing is forbidden, but, well, the Christmas spirit seems to have taken over the house in ways it hasn't in years."

Harriet couldn't help but smile. "That's wonderful to hear."

"What about this one?" Maisie lifted a deep-rose-colored silk evening gown from a pale-blue box.

"Oh, that's far too pretty." Harriet shook her head at the sight of the silken gown that exuded elegant decadence.

"Well, I've got a potato sack down in the kitchen you might prefer."

Harriet's eyes widened, unsure of how to respond. Had the brash comment come because she had somehow caused offense? "P-pardon?"

Maisie covered her mouth as she held back a burst of laughter. "I'm just saying, miss, that you can't spend your life turning down things being offered just because you think they're nice."

"Well, no. I suppose not."

"You should have seen the look on your face just now, miss."

"Well, I'd never heard a servant speak so...boldly before."

Maisie smiled. "Bold? Aye, that's one way to put it. I suppose in any other household I'd have been sacked by now. Mrs. Breland's had words with me on more than one occasion. Course, it's not easy finding people to work here, so that works in my favor."

"Perhaps that's the real reason she approved of Timothy courting you?" Harriet said with a hint of a smirk.

"What do you mean, miss?"

"Well, maybe Mrs. Breland believes that if you're wed Timothy will help keep you in line, become a respectful and dutiful wife?"

Maisie considered this. "Oh, well, aren't they in for a surprise then?"

They both broke out laughing at this, to the point where Harriet had to wipe the tears from her eyes. When their laughter died down, Maisie removed the dress completely from the box and held it up to Harriet.

"I never speak my mind to be rude, miss, but

because I care. This was the second time you tried to refuse something because you thought it looked too nice. Now what does that say about how you see yourself? Nothing good, if you ask me. If you keep saying things like that, sooner or later you'll start to believe them."

"You're right," said Harriet, bowing her head in appreciation. "You have my thanks."

"Now, I'm no expert, but I'd say this is perfect for you. Let's get you dressed for dinner."

Once she was wearing the gown, Harriet stared at her reflection in the mirror. The sheer overskirt carried a dreaminess of romanticism and was embroidered with delicate glittering gold leaves. Heavy satin pink ribbons bordered the hem and made the bottom of the overskirt thick and billowy in a way that would have suited a princess. A matching pink sash around her waist was tightened into a bow at the back, which drew one's eyes to her waist. She looked nervously at the low scooped neckline, and the sleeves of the gown rested on the edges of her shoulders. The décolletage was scandalously low. She'd always worn high-necked gowns at Thursley, fearing what George might say or do if he saw her wearing something so revealing.

"Are you certain they won't fall off?" she asked in a hushed tone as she stared critically at the sleeves.

Maisie fluffed the sleeves into delicate puffs and chuckled. "They won't. The gown's bodice is tight enough. It's designed to rest against the bosom and have the sleeves just barely drape off one's shoulders, like so." The maid plucked at the sleeves, but they remained firmly in place just barely on the edges of her shoulders.

"I've never worn a gown like this before," Harriet admitted.

"Trust me, miss. This gown will do what it was intended to do."

Harriet touched her naked throat and frowned as she pulled on the long white kid gloves. "And what's that?"

"It will draw his eye and show him how lovely you are."

Harriet's belly flipped. "Wait. Was this dress Lord Frostmore's idea?"

"No, miss. It was mine."

"But why?"

"Because His Grace has been thinking terrible things about himself for so long that he's come to believe them. I know what you must be thinking, but I'm not trying to match you, honest. I just think you both need a chance to believe you deserve to have nice things from time to time. Even something as simple as having dinner with an attractive companion."

Harriet considered the maid's words. Did she want the duke to see her as lovely? *Yes.* She did. The realization surprised her. She'd never wanted to feel beautiful before. Beauty had meant danger; it had meant that George would be watching her with those covetous eyes that gave her nightmares. It was different when Redmond looked at her. His hungry gaze excited rather than frightened her. And she realized that Maisie was right—for too long she had denied herself even simple pleasures, and she had begun to think she did not deserve them.

Maisie flashed her a warm smile. "I'll unpack the rest of the clothes for you during dinner."

"Thank you, Maisie. For everything."

As Harriet stepped into the corridor, she heard a distant gong ring out two floors below. She clutched her skirts in one hand and proceeded down to the entry hall. Lord Frostmore waited for her at the bottom stair. He looked exceedingly attractive in his blue superfine coat, gold silk waistcoat, and maroon trousers. His face lit up, and for the first time in her life, she felt the way a woman ought to when she entered a room. That a man's appreciative gaze was a thing to make her shine and not something to fear.

"You look..." He hesitated, and she thought he might be as nervous as she was. "Good, very good."

"Maisie thought you would approve of my wearing these?" She lifted the skirts and waved them a bit.

"She was correct. Besides, they were going to waste where they were. It felt like a crime to let the moths get hold of something so..." He paused, and she saw him ever so discreetly swallow. "Lovely."

"You have wonderful taste, Your Grace. I am honored to wear the dress. I've never worn anything so expensive before."

"Redmond, please call me Redmond." He reached for her hand. "Or Red, if you like. Red was my nickname as a boy. My brother, Thomas, was a few years younger than me and couldn't say Redmond, so he called me Red. I suppose it was because of my hair." He chuckled at the distant memory, and Harriet's spirits lifted.

"Would you call me Harriet then, Red?"

"Harriet." He said her name like he was tasting an expensive brandy and found it to his liking.

They sat down to dinner, the large table set so very far apart, which meant Harriet had to try to speak to Redmond from the farthest end of the table, where a trio of large bouquets kept him almost hidden from view.

"How do you find the dinner?" Redmond's voice

echoed loudly as he almost shouted down the length of the table.

Harriet peered around the edge of the vases, trying to see him better. "I...quite good..."

"What?" he called back and leaned forward in his chair.

"I said, quite good, Your Grace. I think—"

"This is bloody nonsense!" Redmond growled and shoved his chair back quite forcefully, which startled Harriet. Then he collected his goblet of wine and plate and came over to sit down directly beside her. A footman scrambled to collect the duke's silverware and bring it over to them before dashing back into the corner of the room to wait to serve the next course.

"Much better." Redmond looked at her with a grin, and she found herself smiling back at him.

"Indeed."

"I suppose I'll have to tell the footmen to set our plates beside each other at meals. Tradition be damned."

"I would appreciate that." She couldn't help but think back to last night when she had dined with him. How he'd sat at the far end of the table, watching her with dark, hooded eyes, while she'd kept a sword within reach at the table. Not that it had mattered. He'd drugged her and carried her up to his bed, where he'd tended to her wounds with the doctor. How different last night had been compared to this. The man who had frightened her beyond reason was gone. In his place was a man with a kind smile, a guarded heart, and a haunted soul. He was a man she wanted to know everything about.

They dined on soup and salmon, making pleasant conversation throughout the evening.

"Did you enjoy your ride? I saw you from the window earlier. I hope you don't mind—I explored the house for a bit after Mrs. Breland gave me a tour."

"Yes, I did. Riding is one of my favorite pursuits, in addition to reading. Do you ride?"

"When I was a girl, I rode a neighbor's pony once or twice, but until the night of the storm, I'm afraid I hadn't ridden a horse."

"And yet you made it here. Impressive."

"Heavens, I didn't even think. I simply jumped upon the beast and came here. What else could I do?" She blushed and chuckled at herself. Her desire to help Mr. Johnson had overridden all common sense.

"It is as I suspected," Redmond said thoughtfully.

"What is?"

"You are brave. Incredibly so."

"I wish that were the case. But in truth, I'm afraid

of *everything*." It wasn't entirely true, but it seemed like so much had given her cause for fear of late.

"You have no need to be afraid here." Redmond reached out to catch her hand, and the connection sent a tingle up her arm. She didn't pull away. It felt good, more than good, to feel his warm, strong hand on hers.

"Would you tell me about your family and your life here?" She hoped he would open up to her, just as she was opening up to him. She stared at his hand, the long strong fingers, then the way his shoulders strained slightly against the confines of his tailored coat displaying his well-developed body.

Harriet thought again of the contrasting portraits in the hall, the beautiful angelic brother and the duke, who seemed unremarkable by comparison at first. But now it became clear how handsome he truly was. The intelligence in his eyes, the compassion in his features, and the hard-won smiles that seem to burn her body hotter than any of the fires in the great marble hearth behind them. She wanted to know him, to feel that she could call him a friend.

"My family has lived here for three hundred years. We were given these lands by Queen Elizabeth when my ancestors did her a great service. My grandmother told me that the queen even visited us once and stayed in the Pearl Room where you sleep now. We thrive on the wealth of the tenant properties to the north and on investments I made twelve years ago in shipping companies that sail out of Dover. It was how I knew the port would close due to the storms."

"And your family? I know your wife and brother are gone, but what about your parents?"

"My mother died a few weeks after giving birth to Thomas. He was two years younger than me. My father followed her six years later. I was raised to the title of a duke at a very young age and had the help of my father's steward, Mr. Shelton, who resides in London most of the year to look after the estate's interests there." He paused and then squeezed her hand.

"I knew your father, Harriet, though only briefly. He trained me and Thomas one summer when I was just out of university. I liked him very much. I didn't meet your mother, and I am sorry for that." His melancholy smile softened. "If I had continued to work with him, I might have met you. Perhaps I am a villain." He said this last more quietly to himself.

"Why?" She didn't understand.

He looked to her now with a mix of determination and uncertainty. "Because I want you, Harriet. I want things I have no right to have."

She wet her lips with her tongue, afraid and excited all at once. She understood what he meant, but her only experience with desire had been her stepfather's predatory gazes. Redmond was nothing like George, and her body seemed to recognize that.

"That makes you human, Red. We all...want things." Her eyes focused on his lips. For all of his hardness and intimidation that night they first met, his lips had remained soft, inviting, even mocking at times, but their sensual promise had never left them.

"I have a tenuous grip on my lust, Harriet. But I could manage one kiss, if you have no objections."

She didn't have a single one. She leaned closer to him as he cupped the back of her neck and lowered his head to hers. She surrendered to the dangerous promise of life-altering passion he carried with him wherever he went. The desire inside her grew so strong it almost felt like a fury.

Heat uncurled in her abdomen, and she moaned as he parted her lips and his tongue flicked against hers. She hadn't known a kiss could be like this. She felt as though she could leap from the cliffs of Dover, spread her arms, and find white feathered wings that would carry her away upon the winds.

Redmond placed his other hand on her leg, raising her skirts above her knees. She whimpered as he met the bare skin of her inner thighs and tickled her with gentle, exploring fingers. Heat built within her womb, and wetness pooled between her thighs. He deepened the kiss, leaning more over her, and she leaned back in her chair as he continued to touch her.

"I want to devour you," he breathed against her lips. She didn't fully understand his intentions until he pulled her up to her feet and set her on top of the dining room table. The two footmen in the corner of the room scurried out into the hallway and closed the door behind them.

"Red, what are you?"

He silenced her with another kiss. His hands roamed over her body, skimming over her hips. She wanted to feel his palms all over her, touching her in places that seemed to awaken with newly found desires. Harriet sighed against his lips as he held her close, capturing her as he wound his arms around her back, yet she didn't want to be anywhere else in that moment.

"I want you, Harriet. I want to drown in your eyes," he murmured between slow, drugging kisses that made her body sing.

She clutched at his shoulders, feeling his strong, hard muscles beneath her hands. "I want...you too." The heat of his body seeped through the fabric of his shirt.

"Then trust...trust me to give you what you need."

She nodded, and he stole another lingering kiss. Then he lifted her skirts up to her waist, before he lowered her back to lie on the table. Then he bent over her prone body. The wine she'd had with dinner made her dizzy in a good way as he pressed a kiss to her inner thigh and then set his mouth over the most sensitive part of her. If she hadn't been so full of need for his touch, she would have been shocked at the scandalous position they now found themselves in, but she couldn't find it in her to care. She never wanted him to stop what he was doing.

Anticipation pulsed through her as she watched the wicked duke do exactly as he'd promised—give her what she needed. His tongue flitted out against her sensitive folds, and she gasped and moaned and writhed. She closed her eyes and gave over to the sensations of Redmond's mouth on her. His tongue and lips kept her his sweet prisoner as he tortured her.

A building need that she'd never experienced before sent her breath into fast pants, and her vision spiraled. His lips found the small bud of desire within her and sucked on it. She screamed. Pleasure like she'd never felt, frightening and dizzy, hit her like lightning, and her back arched beneath him. His soft laughter cooled her hot flesh as he teased her with his mouth, and then he stroked his hands down her outer thighs and pulled her dress back down. She lay still on her back, panting and trying to understand what had just happened.

"If you"—she breathed hard—"are a villain for that, I may well play your victim anytime you desire."

He laughed and helped her to sit up. She suddenly felt very shy, open, and vulnerable after experiencing such violent pleasure, but he did not give her time to be nervous. He scooped her up in his arms, and they left the dining room. She curled her arms around his neck, taking in his rich scent. She bit her lip to hide a smile at feeling so protected by a man who'd just devoured her in one scandalous moment. He carried her up the stairs to the library, where they settled into an overlarge chair by a healthy crackling fire. He kept her close to him, and she tucked her head beneath his chin as they listened to the logs pop and snap in the hearth.

"You are very brave." He kissed the crown of her hair. "Very brave indeed."

Part of her was still reeling from the pleasure she'd felt in the dining room, but she wanted to speak honestly with him, this man who was in so many ways still a stranger.

"And you are wonderful, Red. *Wonderful*." She wished he could understand that he had given her a precious gift tonight.

He had stripped away her fear of desire. He had

shown her that such intimacy could feel good, could feel safe and yet exciting. It wasn't always frightening, wasn't always fierce looks and greedy hands in the dark. She had the sudden desire to tell him that she wanted to stay here forever, to never sail to Calais, but she couldn't...not unless he asked her to. So instead she breathed and relaxed into him until she fell asleep in the arms of the Devil of Dover.

7

"*Harriet...*" That ethereal voice drew her from sleep again. She opened her eyes and saw lightning flash against the windowpanes. The lamp on the side table burned low, illuminating the pearl-adorned curtains. She was in the Pearl Room, wearing a sheer nightgown of fine silk.

How had she gotten here? Why was she alone? Hadn't she fallen asleep in Redmond's arms in the library? Disappointment settled in a pit in her stomach. She had hoped that Redmond would have stayed with her after what transpired between them.

"*Harriet...*" The mournful call of her name lifted the hairs on the back of her neck.

"Who's there?" she asked, her body shaking as lightning flashed once more and thunder crashed against the manor house, making the bed frame rumble around her.

The pearls winked and sparkled like frozen drops of dew on the black velvet. She blinked, wiping her face with her hands.

Then she saw it. Saw *him*.

A man in the corner was watching her. He was beautiful, but the sight of him filled her heart with such anguish she never wanted to leave. He raised a hand as though to touch her, even though he was across the room.

Harriet couldn't breathe. She clawed at her throat, and the beautiful man, now wreathed in shadows, looked on, watching with sorrowful concern. She reached her hand toward him, gasping for breath.

Then she wasn't in the Pearl Room anymore. She was in another bedchamber. One with more masculine furniture, but it wasn't Redmond's room.

A woman appeared before her, wearing a dressing gown and shawl. She stood facing the man who'd been in her room.

"Do you think he meant it, Thomas?"

She recognized him now. Thomas, Redmond's brother. Harriet watched the man embrace the woman. Love was evident upon their faces. A pure, honest love that made Harriet's heart ache.

"He meant it. Red loves me, and he would do

anything for me." Thomas cupped the woman's face in his hands. "But I've hurt him, Millicent. *We* have hurt him. What we did, what we're doing, is wrong."

"I know, but he agreed to seek an annulment. The scandal will be terrible, but isn't it better to be together? We can face anything." Millicent curled her arms around Thomas's neck, and he stroked her dark hair, cradling her against him.

"I want you," he said to Millicent. "But I cannot lose my brother. He's been like a father to me ever since ours died. I cannot leave him alone after this. Let me speak to him again." Thomas cupped her face and kissed her passionately before leaving the bedchamber.

Harriet, invisible to them as if she were the ghost, was drawn by unseen forces behind Thomas down the corridor to another room. Redmond's room.

"Red?" Thomas eased the door open when no one answered his knock. "Red, please, I need to speak with you." The bedchamber was empty. Thomas quietly slipped down the main stairs and headed toward Redmond's study, but he froze when a cold draft caught his attention. He moved into the main hall, where he caught sight of the open front door. The lightning outside revealed a tall, distant figure. It was Redmond, and he was walking in the direction of the cliffs.

"Millicent! Wake Mr. Grindle and Mrs. Breland. Red's headed for the cliffs!" he shouted back up the stairs, hoping Millicent would hear him.

"What?" Millicent appeared at the top of the stairs. "Oh heavens, I'll wake them at once!" She vanished from sight. Harriet, still bound up in this infernal dream, followed close at Thomas's heels as he raced across the rain-soaked grounds toward the distant cliffs.

"Red!" Thomas shouted as he raced through the violent rainstorm.

"Stop him!" Millicent's cry joined his as Redmond took a decisive step over the edge.

Thomas grabbed Redmond's shirt from behind and pulled him back away from the cliff, stopping him from plummeting to his death.

"Red, what the devil are you thinking?" Thomas demanded, shaking his brother hard.

"Redmond... Don't ever do that again, please." Millicent touched his cheek as she started to cry.

A moment later, the ground beneath their feet shook and crumbled away. Millicent vanished from sight. Thomas and Redmond fell onto the ground, narrowly avoiding her fate.

"Millicent!" Thomas lunged for the edge, but Redmond dragged him back.

"No, you can't." Redmond pinned him to the ground. "She's *gone*."

Suddenly Harriet was drawn into Thomas's head, seeing and feeling what he felt.

Thomas's heart stopped at the words. Time ceased to have meaning. Just moments ago—a lifetime ago—he had believed he would be with her forever, And he had believed that he would find a way to win back Red's trust. And now...the love of his life was dead.

Thomas stared at his brother, wanting to hate him for coming out here. Millicent would still be alive if not for him. But the rage faded as misery overwhelmed it. Red had only come out here to die because of what Thomas and Millicent had done to him.

"I'm sorry," Red murmured. "I'm so sorry."

But Thomas was the sorry one. His gaze turned to the sea, to the battering waves. There was no more light in his world, no more purpose. All had gone dark.

Harriet woke to the sound of a man shouting her name. She blinked, wiped her wet face, and gasped. She saw that she was but a dozen feet away from the cliffs. Icy wind tore at her body, and fresh snow burned her bare feet. How had she gotten out here? Had she followed a phantom to her own doom?

"Harriet!" Redmond's shout startled her. He grabbed her, jerking her into the safety of his arms. He half carried her nearly twenty feet until they were a safe distance from the cliffs. Harriet couldn't stop shaking from the fear and the cold.

"What in blazes were you doing? You could have died!" Redmond growled as he scooped her up in his arms, carrying her freezing form back to the house. Grindle and Timothy met them at the door.

"Have a bath prepared in my chambers at once. And a tray of food and wine."

"Of course, Your Grace." Grindle and Timothy left the pair alone.

"I can walk," Harriet whispered in mortification.

"I'm sure you can, but if it's all the same, I'll feel better keeping you in my arms." Redmond carried her back to his room, and only then did he settle her down in a chair by the fire. She shivered as he covered her with a heavy blanket, then added more logs to the flames. She sensed the tension building inside him.

"What happened, Harriet?" he asked.

She covered her face with her hands. "I... I'm not sure if you would believe me." Only when he gently pried her hands away did she meet his gaze. She wanted to curl up and hug her knees like a small child might, but she couldn't escape the question in his searching face.

"*Please*, Harriet. Tell me. What drove you to want to take your own life?"

"I didn't—" she protested, then drew in a calming breath. "I didn't mean to. I was asleep in my bed, and then I awoke. I heard someone say my name."

"Maisie must have—"

"No," she said, cutting him off. "It wasn't Maisie. The first time... It was *her*. The duchess. She stood behind this very chair and pointed at you while you slept last night. I thought it was merely a strange and fantastical dream, but tonight... *He* came."

Redmond curled his hands around hers as he continued to kneel in front of her. He didn't say anything, but she could see in his eyes that he knew who she meant.

"I woke tonight to find your brother standing in the corner of my room. He terrified me. Suddenly I couldn't breathe, and then I was in his room with the duchess. They were talking about you." She paused, trying to ascertain whether she ought to continue or if it would pain him too much to hear.

"Go on." His face had gone from concerned to still and somber, like a statue.

"They were speaking about how you had found them together. They spoke of a divorce by annulment. Thomas said he'd hurt you and hoped somehow to make amends. He was so upset, Red. I wish you could have seen his face." She couldn't forget Thomas's brokenhearted look.

"I found them in his room that night," Redmond whispered, almost to himself. "I offered Millicent a divorce...and told them I never wished to see them again."

Harriet pulled one of her hands free to touch his face and stroke his hair. The firelight made it look dark and warm as brandy, and the strands were soft and wet beneath her fingertips.

"Thomas went after you to talk and found you on the cliffs."

Redmond nodded and closed his eyes. "I wished to end my life."

"But he stopped you, and Millicent was there. I saw her fall."

His eyes flew open. "How could you have seen all this?"

"I don't know. But he was there, Red, your brother. I think..."

He shook his head. "Don't say it."

"They're both still here." Harriet leaned forward and kissed his forehead, and he dropped his head into her lap, heaving out a deep, shaking breath.

"They cannot be here," he muttered. "Have I not suffered enough without them haunting me?"

"I don't believe in ghosts," Harriet said, "but I must believe what I saw. How else would I know what happened here?"

"Someone could have told you. Mrs. Breland, perhaps."

"You know full well she would not break your trust like that." She gave a gentle tug on his hair, and he lifted his face. For a moment they stared at one another, and she tried to puzzle out the mysteries of this grief-stricken man. He'd been frantic for her, and the wild panic was still there, shadowing his warm hazel eyes. She brushed her hands through his hair, soothing him as best she could, and oddly it calmed her too.

"You should try to sleep, Red." She was worried more about him than herself. Weariness lined his eyes and mouth.

He shook his head. "Not until you're warm and fed."

Later, Harriet emerged from the hot water of the tub and cocooned herself in a dressing gown. She joined Red, and they ate in silence. His face was dark and unreadable as he drank his wine and she hers.

"I should return to my chambers." She rose from her chair, but he caught her arm.

"Wait. Stay here... With me. In my bed." There was no hint of seduction in his eyes. She saw only the raw need to keep her close. She felt the same way.

"Red, I don't think—"

"Please. I will only worry about you if I don't have you in my arms."

Harriet didn't like the idea that she was being seen as an object of pity, but he did want her in his arms, and she readily admitted that she wanted that as well.

He added more logs to the fireplace while she pulled back the covers of his bed. She climbed in, and he settled beside her. Harriet shivered as she realized she was almost naked. He had but to remove the robe she wore...

Redmond brushed her cheek with the back of his hand and touched her shoulder where the robe slid down a few inches to expose it. His eyes gleamed in the dim light, and Harriet wanted nothing more than a moment to forget her fear, to feel safe in his arms, but she also wanted him.

She reached up to part her robe and rolled onto her back. He gazed down at her, at first confused, then surprised, and then, at last, desire glowed in his face, making him beautiful to her.

She curled her hand around his neck and drew his face down to hers. "Please, Red." She didn't need to say anything else. Her mouth met his hungrily. After a moment he moved his mouth down her body, kissing her collarbone, her breasts, his teeth scraping against sensitive skin and nipping until she was hot and flushed. His hands roamed her body, exploring her hips and thighs. She arched and hissed as he slid a finger into her wet folds, but soon she was rocking against his hand.

Harriet clawed at his shirt until he removed it. Redmond moaned as she slid a hand down between their bodies and stroked his erection through his trousers. She tried not to think about how this man seemed to rob her of all good sense, but the need she felt was half physical and half emotional, overpowering everything else.

"Please," she repeated, and he rolled away from her to remove his trousers.

Then he was on top of her, gently parting her thighs. After settling into the cradle of her body, he kissed her fervently as she melted beneath him. He shifted, and she tensed as he started to enter her. But he kissed her again, and before she was ready to worry about it, he thrust inside her. The pinch she felt made her gasp, and she gripped him tightly by the shoulders. He remained still, and she drew deep breaths as she tried to adjust to feeling so full.

"Better?" he asked against her lips.

"Better," she agreed and raised her hips in encouragement.

What followed was the most memorable experience of her life. Redmond joined his body with hers, their mouths fused in a seemingly endless kiss as he claimed her. Harriet never wanted this moment to end. She had tasted pleasure before, but now it was so much more. Her breasts rubbed against his chest and the smattering of hair there. She had never seen that before, the remarkable naked chest of a man. She ran her palms over him, adoring the feel of him beneath her hands. He pushed inside her over and over, the sensation stealing her breath and making her mad with desire. They moved without words, with nothing but the candlelight and the sounds of their breath surrounding them.

Passion for him and other deeper emotions pounded through her blood into her heart as she shattered beneath him. The searing need she'd felt moments before softened into the sweetest sense of contentment. Redmond tensed as he growled her name against her neck and then relaxed into her, a soft look of wonder in his eyes that made her eyes burn with tears. It was as though he hadn't known what they'd shared could be like this. Was what had happened between them so different? Somehow more special than it was with others? Her heart cried out that it was, but she could not speak to it the way he could. Yet she dared not ask him. Instead, she cradled him to her, his head resting against her breasts until he withdrew from her and rolled onto his back.

"Come here," he urged, and she sidled up against him. He tucked her head beneath his chin and wrapped one arm around her waist.

"I must confess something," he said. "It's important that you hear."

She nodded tentatively, unsure of what he meant to say.

"I loved Millicent," he said softly. Her contentment and pleasure at being in his arms quickly faded into the shadows. She tried to pull away, but he held her still, not letting her escape.

"Please listen, Harriet. I loved her, but I think now it was more the *idea* of love that I loved." He sighed, trying to find the right words. "My brother was the fair one, the one with all the charms. I hoped Millicent would love me, would choose me. But she didn't. Her father convinced her that I was the better choice for her family. All along she had loved my brother, but I was so ready for love myself, so ready for a family and happiness that I failed to see she didn't want me. She cared about me, of course, but it wasn't the same as how she felt about Thomas."

Harriet hugged him tightly to her as her heart clenched in pain for him.

"What we have shared in the past few days has been infinitely more than I ever felt with Millicent. That's what I meant to tell you. There's something about you that soothes me. You don't need to ruin a pleasant silence with speaking, but when we talk it's genuine and interesting. You're pure, and I don't mean that in a carnal way. I mean..." Again, he struggled for words. "You speak to me not as a woman who is interested in a duke, but as a man. As myself."

"I understand," she assured him. For some reason, she had never wanted to think about his title. He was her Red. A man who feared love and yet craved it just as strongly. She understood that all too well.

Redmond played with a lock of her hair and held Harriet close as she relaxed into him. For the first time, she felt she could truly rest in this house. Perhaps the ghosts—for she now couldn't doubt they existed and that they were speaking to her—had wanted this. She had felt their love for each other, but also their love for Redmond.

"Red, what happened to Thomas? I saw you save him from falling over the cliffs. How did he die? He didn't show me everything...just what happened on the edge."

"He..." Redmond paused and swallowed audibly.

"He took his own life after we buried Millicent. He couldn't bear to live without her."

"I'm so sorry, Red." She kissed his chin, and he hugged her tighter.

"I never understood before about a man loving a woman with his whole heart, but now... I think I might."

She heard the words, and her heart raced wildly with hope. It was almost a declaration of love. *Almost.* But was love possible for strangers like them? She wished it could be. But he'd lost so much, and she might have to leave for Calais. George wouldn't stop looking for her, and the last thing she wanted to do was put Redmond in any more danger. He may be a duke and have a duke's power, but George was evil, and evil always found a way to hurt good people. She couldn't let Redmond get hurt because of her. That meant she owed him the truth of what she was starting to feel in her own heart.

"I think I might feel the same...about you." She smiled sadly. "I know we barely know each other, but I feel like something fits in place when I'm with you."

Redmond's eyes were warm as he kissed her before he blew out the candle. They fell asleep with the storm outside and the warm fire within.

REDMOND WATCHED THE FLAMES BURN LOW IN THE hearth as his worries plagued him. How was it possible that Thomas and Millicent were still here? They should have shed their mortal coils, yet somehow they'd left some part of themselves behind at Frostmore. What did these ghosts want? Revenge against him? Or were they trying to help him somehow? He honestly didn't know.

"Thomas?" He whispered the name, feeling foolish as he did so.

The curtains at the foot of the bed stirred as if an invisible hand plucked at them. Red held his breath, stunned to see that whatever presence lingered here in his home was trying to communicate with him. It had to be Thomas. They'd shared an unbreakable bond as brothers. If anyone could have found the will to stay behind and watch over him, it would have been Thomas. A thrill shot through him at the thought that he was talking to his deceased brother, yet it also unnerved him. Tonight his brother's phantom had nearly killed Harriet—perhaps not intentionally, but she'd almost died just the same.

"I care about her." He looked down at Harriet. "Please don't risk her life, if you can understand me at all. *Please*." He closed his eyes, almost disbelieving that he was trying to speak with a ghost.

A chilly wind blew the windows open violently.

He left the bed and rushed to the window and latched them shut again. Then he returned to the bed and pulled Harriet closer in his arms.

"Red..." She murmured his name in her sleep, and his heart clenched as a fierce sense of protectiveness swept through him. He knew she had fled from a dangerous home, and he had a feeling that any man who had his eyes set on Harriet would not easily let her go. For the first time in seven years, he was glad that his ghoulish reputation kept people away from Frostmore. But would it be enough to stop whatever ghost haunted Harriet's steps? A ghost not of his making, but dangerous nonetheless.

8

The next few weeks passed in a blur for Harriet. She fell into a comfortable routine of breakfasting with Redmond each morning, and then she and Devil would accompany him on a snowy walk around the grounds of the estate as they were doing now.

She never got tired of watching him play with the imposing yet regal dog. The giant schnauzer would stand perfectly still when Redmond threw a red ball deep into a snowy field until Redmond gave a sharp whistle. Then the dog would dash through the snow, questing for the ball, and upon finding it, he would return it to them.

Devil dropped the ball at Redmond's feet each time and then came to Harriet, who bent and curled her arms around the dog's neck and kissed his furry brow. Devil would start to pant, his pink tongue lolling out of one side of his mouth with sheer delight as he waited for the ball to be thrown again.

"You're spoiling him," Redmond admonished in a teasing tone. "I want him to remain a fierce attack dog. Before you came, he used to delight in chasing women away from my door. I remember one time a young woman and her parents attempted to impose themselves on me. Devil chased them all the way to the gates." Redmond chuckled. "The young woman screamed like a banshee."

Harriet hid a laugh behind her glove. "You're terrible, Your Grace."

Redmond put an arm around her waist and gave her a playful squeeze. "I certainly am."

As they walked back to the house, Harriet looked up at the gargoyles at the gates with different eyes. The menacing faces of the beasts seemed more ancient, more protective than threatening now. Even the house with its turrets and towers, so reminiscent of a medieval fortress, seemed more lonely than frightening. How strange that such strong impressions of a place could change with time. She was glad for it. Frostmore was no longer the foreboding nightmare she'd heard whispers about for so many years. It was a place full of people who longed for love.

"Red... Would we be able to decorate the house for Christmas?"

He arched an eyebrow. "Decorate?"

"Yes, you know, garlands on the banisters, wreaths upon the doors, perhaps even a kissing bough or two?"

His lips slid into a seductive grin. "Suggest a dozen kissing boughs and I'll agree."

Laughing, they entered the house and shed their winter cloaks and gloves, handing them to a waiting footman. Mrs. Breland and Mr. Grindle were conversing about the dinner menu for that evening.

"Ah, good, you're both here," Redmond said as he saw them. "Harriet's had a splendid idea. We should decorate Frostmore for the holidays. What do you think?"

"That is a delightful idea, Your Grace." Mrs. Breland smiled, and Harriet noticed that Mr. Grindle watched her with barely concealed interest. Maisie was right. The butler was infatuated with the house-keeper. Downstairs romances weren't often permitted, but perhaps Harriet could convince Redmond to allow it since his valet had been given permission to court Maisie?

"Excellent. Make what changes you need, and send to the nearby villages for whatever we do not have," Redmond ordered.

"We'll see it done," Grindle promised and gave Harriet a quick smile.

Redmond caught Harriet by the waist. "Well, I have some letters to write in my study. Shall I find you later?"

It had become a ritual for him to find her wherever she was in the afternoon, and more often than not they ended up on the nearest flat surface, clothes scattered about. She couldn't get enough of Redmond or his irresistible touch.

"Yes, please. I'll most likely be in the library." She'd grown obsessed with the vast collection of books he had there.

"Good." He cupped her chin and brushed the pad of his thumb over her lip. The way he stared at her mouth made her tremble and ache. He truly was a wicked man, one who knew exactly how to kindle her darkest desires.

She watched him and Devil head for his study before she ventured into the library. A happy grin spread over her face as she collected several books and sat down to read in her favorite wingback chair by the fire. As she turned the pages, she daydreamed about Christmas at Frostmore and the magic it would bring back into her life and Redmond's. They had both grown so wary of love and trust that neither of them had felt alive in far too long. Her stepfather had turned her from a girl who had enjoyed life into a young woman who feared being used, being *controlled*.

I'm safe here with Red, for now. Safe.

Yet even as she thought the words, she had the eerie sense of something dark and terrible on the horizon, coming for her.

REDMOND SETTLED INTO HIS CHAIR IN HIS STUDY, and Devil sat at his feet, gnawing on a thick bone the cook had saved for him. Redmond ruffled the short-cropped hair on the dog's head before reaching for the nearest stack of letters. The first were several reports on the shipping companies he held interests in based out of Dover, followed by a few from the sheep farmers who had tenant properties on his estate. Finances were tight for the farmers at the moment, so he would move some money from the shipping accounts to tide over the farmers and their families until spring.

The last letter in the stack had a fancy red wax seal. He broke it and unfolded the paper to read the contents. His heart stuttered in his chest, and he crumpled the edges of the paper. A black rage rose up in him like a violent summer storm.

It was a letter from Harriet's stepfather, George

Halifax, and he was searching for his beloved daughter who had stolen his coach and his driver.

How dare this man write to him? They had no acquaintances, no social connections. Redmond read the rest of the letter, his hands clutching the paper tight.

He professed that the young woman was mad, a danger to herself and others. Her mother had recently died, leaving the girl with no one in her life to mold her into respectable feminine behavior after she had become so dangerously willful. George requested that if Redmond knew of her whereabouts to write to him at once so he could come and collect her and bring her home.

The rage that had come upon him so swiftly began to fade as a hint of doubt crept in. Much of what George had said could easily be taken as the truth. Harriet had pulled a sword on him. She'd walked out in the snow in nothing but a nightgown and nearly walked off the cliffs. She not only believed she'd seen ghosts, but she had seen the past through them.

Yet he'd seen the curtains move in his chamber that night they'd first made love. He'd felt that unnatural chill associated with the spirit world and had sworn he caught a fleeting glimpse of his brother. But everything he had experienced could be dismissed with rational explanations, whereas her experiences could not be explained. The edge of doubt remained, a sliver of whispering darkness in his mind.

Redmond stared at the page a long time, weighing what he'd come to know of Harriet against the claims in the letter. He had, luckily, one more witness to ask on the matter. He set the note down and left his study, Devil following on his heels. He entered the service area belowstairs, startling his poor cook and sending two footmen and a scullery maid dashing out of his way. He found Mr. Johnson in the servants' dining hall, finishing his noonday meal. The man had remained here at his estate, along with George's coach, while the driver's broken leg healed.

"Your Grace." Mr. Johnson reached for his crutches, which were leaning against the edge of the table next to his half-eaten soup and bread.

"Please, stay seated. I have a few questions for you."

Mr. Johnson waited, his hands fluttering in his lap as he toyed with his napkin. "I'll answer as best I can."

"I need only the truth. Nothing you say will have you removed from my home, nor have you face any other trouble. Is that understood? You may speak freely without fear of repercussions."

"I understand, Your Grace," the driver answered.

"Harriet's stepfather, George Halifax. What sort of man is he?" When Mr. Johnson hesitated, Redmond encouraged, "The truth, please."

"He's not the best of men," Mr. Johnson began. "He has a sharp tongue, and he's been known to strike a servant a time or two."

"And what of Harriet and her mother? How did he treat them?"

"He was nice enough at first, I suppose, like lots of men are when they want something. Miss Emmaline was such a sweet lady, but she had a desperate look about her. Mr. Halifax saw that and took advantage. Miss Harriet was still a girl when she and her mother moved in. Thursley was bigger than anywhere they'd ever lived before, and they weren't used to being waited upon. It was rather nice, the way they thanked us downstairs staff for anything we did." Mr. Johnson's face reddened. "Not to say I needed that. It's my job, after all, but it's nice to be appreciated for hard work once in a while."

He cleared his throat before he continued. "Well, after a year or so, my master started to show his true self. Miss Emmaline was able to handle him, even the few times he struck her, but she was more worried about Harriet. You see, when Miss Emmaline married my master, he convinced her to sign a guardianship agreement. Until Harriet's twentieth birthday, he has full rights over her. That was meant to protect her, but recently the house realized it also meant he could control her, hurt her, starve her, prevent her even from escaping by marriage. All without consequence. The staff did their best to look out for her. The cook would put a light sleeping draft in the master's food to make him tired on those nights when she saw the evil gleam in his eyes."

Redmond could barely contain the rage bubbling inside him. A wave of self-loathing followed as he recalled how he had tried to frighten Harriet. He had been no better than her stepfather, though he'd had no intention to hurt her, let alone ravish her. But she hadn't known that.

"Do you believe he will come after her?" Redmond asked Mr. Johnson.

"Yes. I'm surprised he hasn't tracked us here already. I knew the moment I helped Miss Russell escape him that I would lose my employment there. He will no doubt accuse me of stealing the coach and have me imprisoned."

"Mr. Johnson, consider yourself under my employment. Once you're healed, your duty will be to watch out for Miss Russell." He started to go but paused and asked the driver one last thing. "When does she turn twenty?" Redmond wished Harriet had trusted him sooner with all of this. He could have been taking measures to protect her. As a duke he had some power, but he wasn't sure he could override a guardian without facing a magistrate.

"January seventh, Your Grace."

"Thank you, Mr. Johnson." The driver bowed his head as Redmond left. He had to find Harriet, if only to assure himself that she was safe. As he entered the great hall, he couldn't shake the feeling that he was being watched. But not by living eyes...

"Thomas, please," he murmured, feeling foolish again for talking to the air. As the feeling began to fade, he exhaled in relief. He had a real, living, breathing demon now to defend against. He could not afford to worry about ghosts in the shadows.

HARRIET HAD FELT THOSE SPECTRAL EYES UPON HER again. She shivered, but when she looked up, she saw only Redmond watching her, not a ghost. Her body began to hum as she noticed the intensity of his gaze.

She put her book down and started toward him. "Red?"

The duke acted fast, grasping her waist and pinning her against the nearest bookcase. He held her tightly to him, one hand wound around her back and the other fisting gently in the coils of her hair as he inhaled her scent and kissed her neck.

"I'm glad I found you," he said. His words sounded odd, as though he had not expected to find her at all. It made her wonder if that was indeed what he meant.

What had begun as a gentle hold turned harder for both of them. The bookshelf creaked as Redmond pressed her against it, and she gasped as bolts of arousal shot through her. The duke's desire was evident, but she was too short for him to easily reach down to kiss her mouth. She tried to curl one leg around his waist and cursed her cumbersome skirts. She dug at his coat, pulling it off him as he playfully nipped her shoulder.

She loved his possessive grip on her body as he lifted her up and set her down on the ledge of the bookshelf. He hiked up her mauve silk skirts to her waist so she could part her legs. Redmond was an excitement she had never imagined possible. Her hands tangled in his flaming hair as she quested for deeper kisses. Redmond groaned against her mouth, and his hands drifted down her back to her backside. He clenched her hard, urgently, pulling her tightly to him.

"I want you, Red," she whispered frantically. "*Here*." She didn't care if anyone saw them. All she knew was that she wanted his body against hers. He dropped a hand to the front of his trousers as she pushed aside her underpinnings.

His eyes were the color of wheat fields, burning with a golden intensity as he stepped into the cradle of her thighs and slid one hand down to her core. He stroked her with his fingertips, teasing her until she wanted to scream at him for not being inside her.

"Please, you're teasing me," she growled, and he shifted his hips, penetrating her now, filling her up.

She moaned, her head falling back as he withdrew and thrust back into her. She bucked against him, delighting in their almost violent union, and she reveled in the pleasure that seemed to rebound between them. Redmond breathed hard as he plunged deep and fast. It almost hurt to feel him enter her over and over with such vigor, but she liked the exciting edge of uncertainty that came with making love to him. He was a man of intensities: intense passion, intense tenderness. Yet she knew he would never hurt her. She spread her legs more, clinging to him as he claimed her relentlessly. Then she pulled his mouth back to hers, her arms twining about his neck as he rocked back and forth.

The shelf behind her shifted with the force of their lovemaking. His hard length filled her, prolonging her desire to come. His strength was all-encompassing, his passion beyond words. It was like she was making love to a sun god, not a dark devil. He was all fire and pleasure. She gave in to the sinful force of their bodies colliding and could not imagine ever leaving him.

Redmond's eyes glinted as he stared down at her, knowing full well the pleasure he was giving her. It only made him move faster, filling her body with his. His rough and possessive drive threw her over the edge into sizzling sensations of obliterating pleasure. She cried out. He covered her mouth with his, swallowing her scream and kissing her until she was quivering, feeling only the sensations of pleasure rioting through her body.

He gasped, holding her tightly as his muscles went rigid. Then he seemed to recover, and he rocked inside her, tender and sweet now as he pressed kisses to the crown of her hair. Her body clenched around him as aftershocks of pleasure made her womb tighten. She wrapped her arms around his shoulders as he shuddered, his body trembling almost as hard as hers. She wanted to hold him and never let go.

Her breath was shaky as she placed soft kisses against his neck. He stroked her hair, the ferocity of their almost frantic coupling settling into the sweetest of moments. The duke, with all of his near brutal seduction, was a masterful lover, and she was bound to him now, bound by adoration and fascination. She realized then—as he stole a deep, lingering kiss that made her toes curl—that she was falling in love with him.

You fell in love with him weeks ago, a voice murmured inside her head. She could not find a way to deny it.

When Redmond withdrew from her, she missed him instantly. He fixed his trousers and then put her dress to rights before he lifted her up off the shelf and set her on her feet. She almost collapsed into him on her shaky legs.

"Sorry," she said shyly.

"Don't apologize. A man likes to think he's a good lover, and when he leaves a lady weak-kneed, that's solid proof." He caught her hand and pulled her toward one of the fainting couches near the windows and lay down, pulling her on top of him. She almost protested at the intimate position, but considering how they'd just made love against a bookshelf in the middle of the day...

His lashes fluttered down as he sighed and relaxed beneath her. She shifted to tuck herself in between the side of the couch and his body. He wrapped an arm around her, and she laid her cheek against his chest. The slow, steady beat of his heart was an unexpected intimacy. She stole one more look at him, counting the ghost of freckles upon his nose and cheeks in the bright winter sunlight.

"You should rest," he said with a small chuckle. Blissful delight moved through her as slow as molasses, and she grinned sheepishly, even though his eyes were still closed and he couldn't see.

"Red..." She spoke his name tentatively. "Can I stay with you?"

"Stay?"

"Yes. I don't know what awaits me in France. I was so desperate to escape before, but now I feel safe here with you. I don't want to leave in the spring." She held her breath, knowing how very mad she was to beg him like this. "You don't need to change anything. I don't expect... I just wish to stay, in whatever way you would let me."

He opened his eyes. "You would be content to be my secret lover?"

She drew in a deep breath. "As long as I can love you, that is all I require."

He cupped her cheek and sighed. "You truly are the sweetest little creature I've ever met. Where were you seven years ago? Why couldn't it have been you?" he uttered, his voice a little hoarse. She understood. Seven years ago, he'd pledged his heart to another woman, and he'd been hurt. Betrayed. He wished he could go back; it was clear in his eyes. He couldn't erase the years that had passed by or banish the ghosts in the shadows.

"Sleep," he said.

She laid her head on his chest, fighting tears over the fact that he hadn't said she could stay. She would give him time, and she would wait to see if he changed his mind.

Just as she closed her eyes, surrounded by the warmth of his body and the sunlight streaming through the windows, she thought she heard him whisper, "Perhaps I will keep you."

❧ 9 ❧

Harriet wasn't sure how long she had slept, but when she woke, she was alone on the fainting couch. Redmond must have draped a blanket over her and cradled her head with a soft blue velvet pillow. Redmond's scent was still there, that faint hint of the woods and snow. She breathed in deeply and blinked slowly, rubbing her eyes with her fists.

She was usually such a light sleeper, so she was surprised that she hadn't woken when Redmond had slipped her off his body. Where had he gone to? He probably had more ducal estate matters to concern himself with, but nevertheless, she *missed* him.

Stretching her limbs, Harriet dropped the blanket from her body and took stock of her appearance. Her gown was dreadfully wrinkled, and her hair was quite mussed, but did it matter? No one was here to see her or judge her other than the servants, and she knew that they liked her. More importantly, they liked her being with Redmond. Their time together was changing him for the better. Mrs. Breland had confessed the previous week that he was finally starting to act like the man he'd been seven years ago. That thought alone made Harriet's heart fill with joy.

Harriet felt wonderful, spectacular, better than she had ever felt before in her life, though that probably had something to do with their rough-and-tumble lovemaking against the bookshelf. She bit her lip to stifle a fit of giggles when she noticed the massive pile of books that had fallen off the top shelf. Their lovemaking *had* been earth-shattering.

She climbed off the fainting couch and walked over to try to clean up the chaos. After putting the books away, she stepped back and looked at the shelf in satisfaction. No one would guess what she and Redmond had done here. She exited the library to find Devil waiting for her just outside.

"Well, hello there. Are you looking for Redmond?"

Devil rose from a seated position, holding a long knotted piece of rope, and then he crouched defensively, clearly ready to play.

"Oh, I see. Redmond is busy, and so you've come

looking for me." Harriet laughed, catching the end of the rope and tugging it hard. Devil thrashed his head back and forth, trying to shake her hold free, just as he did with Redmond. After several minutes, Harriet was breathless as she let him at last have his triumph and pull the rope free of her hand.

He trotted to the far end of the corridor and paused to eye the end of a runner rug before he dug furiously in an attempt to bury the rope. Then he returned to her, a decidedly smug canine expression on his face, as though he was convinced he'd successfully hidden the rope from her. He continued to follow her around the house as she explored Frostmore room by room once again. It was a vast house, with many darkened chambers and locked doors. Servants bustled around her when she came upon them, and they offered warm smiles. She'd come to fit into life at Frostmore in the last few weeks.

Harriet paused in the long picture gallery, admiring Redmond's portrait. She preferred the real duke in person, but while he was busy in his study, she found this portrait of him comforting. She shook her head and looked down at Devil.

"I am unaccustomed to wishing to be with someone so much, especially a man." She scratched the dog's folded ears, which felt soft as velvet. She felt like she could confess anything to her attentive companion. "I'm in love with him, you see, and when I'm with him I feel strong and brave. Does that make me silly?"

The dog cocked his head to one side, as if considering her question. Then his tongue flopped out of his mouth, destroying the thoughtful expression.

"Not so silly, then?" The dog barked once, and she giggled. "Where is your master? In his study, I suppose. Does daylight offend his demon sensibilities?" She'd come to call him her demon lover sometimes, because he had been so wicked upon their first meeting, and now... She was spellbound by his carnal hungers and couldn't resist teasing him for them.

Devil licked her hand.

"Let's go bring him some tea and biscuits." She gave Redmond's portrait a lingering look before they left the hall of Redmond's ancestors. She felt a dozen gazes coming through the centuries of painted oil faces as she passed them by. She only hoped the ghosts caught within the canvases would find her worthy of Redmond.

REDMOND HELD THE LETTER FROM GEORGE Halifax again, staring down at the words that had sent him running to find Harriet a few hours ago.

Then he cast it into the hearth across from his desk and watched it burn.

Grindle appeared in his study doorway. "Your Grace... You have a visitor."

"Oh?" Redmond straightened in his chair. He wasn't expecting anyone. "Who?"

"Mr. George Halifax." Grindle's somber expression warned Redmond that Grindle recognized the name and was as displeased as Redmond was to hear it. He'd shared with Grindle just a short while ago that Halifax was Harriet's stepfather and that Redmond didn't trust the man at all. He'd confided in Grindle that he could even pose a danger to Harriet.

"Bring him to me. But first, find Harriet. Take her to my bedchamber and keep her there. I do not want him to know she is here."

"A wise decision, Your Grace." The butler left, and Redmond rubbed his temples as his head began to ache behind his eyes. All he wanted was to be back with Harriet in the library. He regretted leaving her sleeping so sweetly without him. When they had lain there together, she had snuggled up against him so tenderly, it was as though she meant to keep him as close to her as she could. Whenever he'd taken Millicent to bed, she'd always wished to return to her chamber afterward. It had wounded him to be denied the intimacy of holding her in his arms, feeling connected. Now he had found that connection with Harriet, and if he wasn't careful, it could all be stolen from him.

George Halifax was soon shown into Redmond's study. The man was tall and muscular, but fairly thick and most likely not in peak physical condition. Redmond couldn't help but measure himself against the man, and he decided with certainty that he could best him in any form of combat. He stood up and nodded for Halifax to take a seat.

"Thank you for agreeing to see me, Your Grace. I know we have not been formally acquainted, and I hate to impose upon you, but I sent you a letter a few days ago. Did you receive it?"

"I did, though I confess I only just read it this morning."

"So you know that it concerns a grave matter. My ward, Miss Russell, is missing. Her mother has passed away, and I find myself in the position of being Miss Russell's sole guardian. I have been worried sick over her whereabouts. You are a bastion of strength to Dover. I knew I could trust you to help me once you heard of my plight." Halifax's expression was earnest and open, but Redmond had learned long ago that people could pretend to be something they weren't. Still, even if the man was full of lies, those lies might unwittingly reveal a truth.

"I am listening, Mr. Halifax."

"I married Miss Russell's mother six years ago and raised her daughter as my own. She was a willful child, and while I admire spirit in young ladies, it was clear my Harriet was far more spirited than is tolerable."

Redmond curled his hands into fists beneath his desk when Halifax said "my Harriet," but he let the man continue.

"Her mother fell ill and has only just passed away, but before she died, Harriet ran away and stole my coach and driver in the process. Her mother wished for me to continue as her guardian until after her birthday, but I fear it may have to be longer than that. She is vulnerable, and I believe prone to fits of madness."

"Fits of madness?" Redmond asked quietly.

Halifax's tone turned graver still. "Yes. She's capable of violent outbursts and spinning fantastical tales. To run away from the shelter of my home while her mother lay dying? That is proof enough to me that she needs special care. I only wish to have her back under my roof to protect her from herself."

The man was a remarkable actor. If Redmond hadn't had the instinct so deeply ingrained in him to mistrust people's motives, he would have been tempted to believe Halifax over Harriet.

"I put my faith and trust in you, Your Grace, that you would tell me if she was here."

Redmond didn't miss the slight hint of an accusation in Halifax's words. He must have suspected that the only logical place a woman could find shelter in the surrounding area would be his home. He was tempted to call Halifax out for suggesting he would lie, but he *was* going to lie about Harriet.

"I would, but she is not here. I do, however, have your coach and your driver." Redmond thought quickly on his feet. "We encountered the vehicle broken down upon the road a few weeks ago. He made mention of helping your stepdaughter, but he said the moment the coach overturned she abandoned him. He suffered a broken leg, and a doctor from nearby has been assisting in his recovery. He is still not able to move on his leg and must continue to convalesce here a few more weeks, but I can have your coach horses ready to leave in an hour if you wish to take them home. I would have contacted you sooner, Mr. Halifax, but my business has kept me away, and I have only just returned to learn of the incident this morning from my butler."

Halifax nodded, as if Redmond's excuse was quite believable. "I would be glad to take the coach and horses now, and I trust if my daughter appears on your estate, you will take the necessary steps to return her to my care?"

Redmond wanted to punch the man so hard his jaw broke, but the game was still afoot, so instead he smiled and held out his hand to shake Halifax's.

"Of course. She sounds quite disturbed and would benefit from a firm, caring hand."

"Thank you, Your Grace. In the meantime, I have already begun the paperwork to have her declared disturbed. The magistrate in Faversham will be signing the papers any day now." Halifax smiled, and this time, a bit of his true desires slipped out. A hint of a triumphant gleam lingered a moment too long in his eyes.

"My man, Grindle, will show you out now."

Halifax exited the study, and Redmond sank back in his chair, a knot of concern tightening in his stomach. He had no doubt that Harriet was still in danger, now more than ever. He didn't trust Halifax to stay away from his lands. It was clear from the man's sharp gaze that he thought Redmond was lying. Halifax had likely searched both Dover and Faversham already. Frostmore was the most logical choice for a woman to hide. That meant Harriet wasn't safe here. She would never be able to leave the grounds, possibly not even the house. She would slowly wither away from being closed off from the world like that. The thought that had lingered darkly at the edges of his thoughts now returned and was unavoidable. Harriet could not stay. She needed to leave, to go somewhere permanently out of Halifax's reach.

Or she could stay...if you weren't such a coward to marry again, a dark voice whispered inside him.

But it was the truth. He was afraid to marry again, afraid to tie his life to another person's after the betrayal he'd suffered the last time. What if he was wrong about how Harriet seemed to feel about him? What if she didn't love him the way he hoped to be loved? He couldn't bear to have another Millicent situation; this time there wouldn't be anyone to stop him from stepping off the cliffs and answering that frightening call of the void and the death that would follow.

If she stayed and he married her, he'd face legal ramifications in the courts, but at least Harriet would be his. But it would be easier—and safer for his heart —to send her far away from here where she could be free of her stepfather.

And I can go back to being alone.

A deep ache settled inside his chest as he left his study. He heard Grindle say goodbye to Halifax, and he waited just out of sight until the door closed.

"Did you find Harriet?" he asked.

"Yes, Your Grace. She is in your room."

"Thank you." He paused. "Have a groom trail that man's coach as far as he can without being seen. Have him stick to the woods if possible, then return. I wish to know if Mr. Halifax takes any detours."

"Yes, Your Grace."

Redmond hurried up the stairs and burst inside his chambers. Harriet stood ready to fight, a fencing blade at the ready and Devil by her side.

"Oh, heavens, Red, you frightened us! We heard footsteps on the stairs and thought..."

Redmond came to her and gently removed the sword from her hand and let it clatter to the floor. Devil barked once and then trotted over to the carpet by the fireplace and settled down, resting his head on his paws.

"It's all right. He's gone." Redmond wrapped his arms around Harriet, stunned at how the strong, brave woman only drew out his fiercely protective side.

She buried her face in his neck. "I cannot go back, Red. You don't know what he's like." She whispered the words so softly it seemed as if he might've imagined them.

"I know." He brushed a hand down her back and cupped her head with his other hand, feeling her golden hair like sunlight warming his fingertips.

"You do?"

"Mr. Johnson warned me about him this morning. He told me about Halifax. Harriet... Your mother is gone. Halifax told me she passed."

She burrowed deeper into his arms. "I knew it. I sensed it, the way a heavy storm finally clears and pale watery skies replace the gloom. I couldn't feel her pain in my heart anymore." She sniffled. "There's a bleak emptiness there instead."

"You *aren't* empty," Redmond reassured her. Once, long ago, he'd dreamed of being close like this to his wife, to offer comfort and love, yet he had never been given the chance. And now Harriet, the woman who could have offered him so much, the woman he could have given anything to, could not belong to him.

"What if he learns I'm here?" She pulled back to look up at him. "I won't be safe anywhere. He's not afraid of anything."

"You think he'd come onto my lands to try to hurt you while I'm here?"

Harriet answered with a slow nod, her eyes full of a weariness that worried him more than he wished to admit.

"Even if I stayed here, and had all the protection a duke could offer, I don't think it would be enough, Red. He won't stop coming after me, and I don't want to put you or the staff here at risk."

He wanted to disagree, to tell her that she was

safe, but it would be a lie, and he didn't want any lies between them.

"You're right. He's a dangerous man. The only way to keep you safe is for you to go. You must leave tomorrow morning. We'll ride to Dover and find you a ship. The Channel has not yet become too treacherous for a winter crossing. I'll see to it you have money for clothes and food. You'll have plenty to set yourself up with in Calais or Normandy where your father's family is."

Harriet's eyes filled with unshed tears. "You want me to leave?"

"I would give *anything* for you to stay. But fate has other plans, I fear. I don't trust Halifax either."

"Even having escaped him, George has managed to out-fence me," she muttered. "He has still won, even if he does not possess me, because he has denied me happiness, and I must leave the second place in my life that truly felt like home."

"Yes, you must," Redmond agreed. "He means to prove you are mad or disturbed so as to retain guardianship over you, even after you would have legally escaped him. He's already begun the paperwork with the magistrate in Faversham."

Fresh terror struck her face. "Oh Lord, Red."

He held her fast, not letting her go as she trembled again in his arms.

"We'll arrange with Grindle and Mrs. Breland for you to leave tomorrow." The words felt bitter upon his tongue.

She was quiet a long moment before she raised her face to his. "Red, I don't want to leave."

"You must." *Even if it kills me to let you go*.

She tried to pull away, to turn her back, but he wouldn't let her. Instead he gathered her close again. Her slender hands twisted anxiously before they settled on his chest. Misery tore through him, leaving an emptiness inside his heart, except for a faint glow that she'd kindled weeks ago from a dying fire.

"I could arrange for you to have a home in France, but I couldn't come to you, not right away. He will have eyes following me, I'm certain of that."

"No, you cannot do that. He could find out somehow. Better if I go alone with no connection between us."

Her words, even though they were meant to protect them both, burned like a hot poker against his heart.

"I will fight him in the courts. I have influence over the magistrate in Dover, and I'm certain that with time, I could gain enough power in Faversham to find a way to reverse whatever ruling the judge makes if it's in Halifax's favor. I'll need time, time where I can know you're safe, far away from him."

"Oh please, Red." Her tormented tone pulled at him, and he knew that if he did not kiss her one last time he might perish. So he defied the agony and pain that formed an invisible shroud inside him and stole another kiss.

"We have but the fading daylight left, my darling." He brushed his nose against hers before pressing his lips to hers, soft but urgently. A powerful sense of awakening from a very long, terrible dream stole over him, one that had held him trapped for seven years.

Harriet kissed him back, her youthful passion and sweet ardor like a flash of brilliant light. It reminded him of when he had been a lad roaming in the attics. When he'd gotten bored, he'd thrown a few stones around and shattered a dust-covered window. The explosion of light had blinded him. It had been the single most glorious experience of his life, to feel the bright sun burning his body, reminding him of the joys of being alive, being outside and living in the world.

"Harriet," he murmured against her lips. "Against the will of my hesitant heart, I have fallen in love with you."

He didn't want to go another moment without having said these words. Yes, he would lose her. Yes, he would never find this feeling again with anyone else, but at least he would have said it. At least he would know that she felt the same.

Her blue eyes were soft like a sunny summer sky. "I love you too. More than is wise, but I love you all the same." Her melancholy smile echoed his own pain.

It was all that needed to be said between them as he carried her to his bed.

They took their time undressing each other. He memorized the slopes and curves that made her unique, that made her exquisite perfection. She was his light in the gloom, the piece of his life he'd thought lost years ago.

Redmond laid her down beneath him, covering her face with kisses. He savored her shivers and sighs as he kissed his way down her body. She giggled as he nibbled on one nipple and then the other. Her hands dug through his hair in a way that made his entire body go rigid with pleasure. She scraped her nails down the back of his neck, which made him groan. Then he placed kisses on her stomach as he made his way down between her legs. She had become less shy these past few weeks, and he enjoyed how free she seemed to be with him, their passions equal to one another.

Now skin to skin, two joined as one, he entered her gently. It was an exquisite torture to make love to her like this, yet it felt like heaven. She locked her legs around his waist as she pulled his head down to hers.

"I never tire of kissing you," she breathed. Love and honesty glowed in her eyes, and it humbled him to his core. He shivered above her as he withdrew and sank back into her welcoming heat.

"In all my life," he whispered, "there has never been anyone like you, nor will there be again." Then he kissed her, deep, slow, his tongue playing an ancient game with hers.

The turbulence that had ruled his life for the last seven years had suddenly stilled into this most perfect moment of calm. Yet he was full of energy, full of joy, full of love, so strong his heart felt fit to burst. Their gentle rhythm quickened over time as their frantic need to taste each other, to share the pleasure of their love, grew stronger.

He delighted in drawing small gasps of excitement from Harriet as he claimed her. Redmond's own breath shortened as he came close to the edge. He slid a hand between their bodies, finding her bud of arousal and circling his finger over it until she arched beneath him and her inner walls clamped down around his shaft.

Then he was lost, his heart and soul pouring out of him and into her, and coming back again. A long moment later, he covered their bodies with the coverlet before pulling her to his side. He kissed her forehead and held on to her, closing his eyes.

If love was a heavy tome in his library, every page would have Harriet's face sketched upon it and poems about her written in a dozen languages. It would contain life's most powerful secrets, transcendental and far too enlightened for a soul like his. Yet if that book did exist, he would vow to read every page every night for the rest of his life until he was an old man, watching the sun set a final time. That way, he would never lose the memory of her. Harriet would be with him always.

Then he would be able to tell the ghosts that breathed within the walls that he had done one good thing with his time upon this earth. He had loved Harriet more than his own life, and he had been loved in return. There was no greater gift than that, and he would lose it forever come the dawn.

🌱 10 🌱

Harriet buried her sorrow deep within her heart as she closed the valise Maisie had packed full of beautiful gowns. Gowns fit for a duchess. They didn't belong to her, but Redmond had insisted they belonged only to the Duchess of Frostmore.

He cupped her face and leaned in to whisper, "In my heart, there will be no other. You are *my* duchess."

She hadn't been able to deny him anything. He stole more kisses, his eyes rimmed with red as he dragged his hands through his hair as if he longed to pull the strands out in frustration.

She wrapped her arms around his neck, not caring that the staff were watching her. They had all come to say their goodbyes.

"Thank you for giving me a place to belong. A

home." The words burned her throat, and she could barely speak. "Thank you for letting me love you." Whatever fate held for her now, she had been given the most precious gift a person could ever have. The gift of his love.

He wiped at her dry cheeks as she managed a bright smile. "No tears?"

"One cannot cry when one realizes one has been blessed beyond all measure." She stepped away from him, the action cutting her heart, but she dared not let him see how much. Instead, she knelt by his side to pet Devil, who watched in silence. As always, the dog seemed to sense her moods, and his brown eyes were heavy with reciprocal pain. She threw her arms around the dog's neck and hugged him tight, then stood and looked at Redmond again.

"You won't see me to Dover?" she asked again, needing as much time as she could with him before saying goodbye.

He shook his head, a rueful smile on his lips. "If I went, there is no way I would be able to stand by and let you board a ship."

She understood, even though it hurt. Better to make a clean break of it here where it still felt less real.

"Write to me once you're safe." His quiet request

startled her. It would pain them both, but she would do as he asked.

"And you?" she asked. "You'll not go back into hiding? You promise to do as I asked?"

He nodded. That morning, as they had lain in bed, watching the pale sunlight stretch across the bedchamber, she'd made him vow not to hide from life any longer.

She touched his cheek one last time with a gloved hand, and he caught her wrist, holding it against his face for a long moment, their eyes locked.

Then he whispered hoarsely, "Go now... or I will lose the courage to let you go."

She turned and rushed out the door and hastened down the steps into the waiting coach. If she looked back, she knew it would break her soul, not just her heart. Redmond's driver helped her inside, and she leaned back against the seat cushions and drew in a shuddering breath as the coach began to roll away.

It was early evening as they reached the port, and she tried to keep herself busy by thinking about what she would do once she reached Calais.

"We're here, miss." The driver offered her his hand as she stepped down. The Port of Dover was quiet; only half a dozen vessels were docked. Their masts looked like an ancient forest, dead and quiet.

Somewhere a bell clanged, and a man called out the change of an evening watch aboard one of the vessels.

"I'll go and see which boat you can book passage on," the driver said, and he headed into the nearest shipping office.

Harriet waited, her cloak hood pulled up against the chill. She watched the men on the ships in the distance as they saw to their duties.

Suddenly someone grabbed her shoulder, and something hard dug into her back.

"Not one scream, dear daughter," George hissed from behind her. "Not one, or I'll sink this blade into you."

Fear enveloped her as she closed her lips and nodded.

"Good. Move backward with me." He pulled her along until she was almost falling, then she was spun around to face his coach waiting in the shadows. George shoved her hard, and she stumbled inside. She tried to rush through to the other door to escape, but the two ghoulish men from his home were there, and they grabbed her, one pinning her arms to her sides and the other smothering her mouth with his hand.

"Bind her wrists and gag her," George snapped.

Harriet struggled, clawing and kicking, till George's knifepoint pricked her chest, cutting through the rose-colored gown she wore. She stilled, and the men on either side of her bound her hands. One balled up a bit of cloth and forced it between her lips.

Unable to resist, she cast her gaze out the window of the coach, hoping Redmond's driver might see her. But her last hope failed her, and she sank defeated back against the seat.

"Do you have any idea the trouble you've caused me, little Harriet? Faversham has been flapping with gossiping tongues about where you've run off to. Your little adventure has brought shame upon my name and my home. You'll pay dearly for it, and Lord Frostmore won't be able to hide you this time."

Her eyes widened at Redmond's name, and it didn't escape his notice.

"Oh, I knew you were there. It was only the only place close enough, and it was too cold for you to be in the woods for long. It's quite clear that you're mad. Why else would a young woman run to a notorious wife murderer for help? Luckily for you, we have a doctor waiting at Thursley to declare you disturbed, and I have a local magistrate preparing to sign papers to the effect as we speak. Then I shall have a guardianship over you for the rest of your life. How long that is depends on whether or not you please me."

Harriet stared at him. Horror filled her until she felt nothing else. This man was a true devil, hidden behind a mask of caring and decency. She had hoped he would forget her in time, but his obsession ran too deep.

"Don't look at me like that," he snapped. "I rescued you from a murderer."

Of course he would paint himself the hero, rescuing her from the Devil of Dover, but he was the only devil in this tale.

"If you remain sensible, you may have the gag removed." He nodded to one man, who pulled the cloth from her mouth. They must be too far from Dover now for him to worry about her screaming. "We won't make it back to Faversham tonight. I have a room secured at an inn nearby. We shall sleep and proceed to Thursley tomorrow."

"One room?" Harriet asked, her voice cold, her body still numb.

George smirked. "Of course. I can't very well leave you alone in your own room. Not in your condition. We wouldn't want anything to happen to you."

She swallowed down a wave of nausea and tried to clear her thoughts. She would have to be smart, play as though he'd defeated her. Once his guard was down, she would fight to the death to win her freedom again.

"I can see you plotting and scheming, my dear. Whatever you're planning, it won't work."

The rest of the journey, George talked about his grand plans, how he would wait a respectable amount of time before marrying her, scandal be damned. She was, after all, only his ward and not his daughter. Harriet allowed herself to escape deep within her mind. She was back in Frostmore, exploring the old house, walking through the snow-covered grounds, running to Redmond and throwing herself in his arms. George could never lay claim to these memories. They were hers alone.

They reached the inn just after nightfall, and George told the innkeeper that they would take their meal in their room. Harriet sat across from him at the small table, eating reluctantly. She wondered if George would drug her, but she knew he would enjoy her screaming in pain and would likely prefer her to be fully aware of her powerlessness when he took advantage of her. He was obsessed with possessing and controlling her, the sort of man every woman feared, even the bravest ones.

George finished his meal and reached forward to clasp her hand where it lay on the table. She tried to pull away, but his grip tightened hard enough to leave red marks.

"I want us to be friends, Harriet."

"And I want you to let go of me." She tried to keep her tone polite.

He rose from his chair and came to stand behind her. He stroked her loosely coiled hair, then dug his hand into it sharply, forcing her head back to look up at him. His other hand clamped around her throat.

"My dear sweet Harriet, do not anger me. I only wish to still that wild spirit in you. It will do you no good to fight." He loosened his hand on her throat just as her vision started to go black. She coughed violently as she gasped for air. But he wasn't done with her. He jerked her to her feet and moved her toward the bed.

"Come over here and rest. You may sleep soundly knowing that I will be here to watch over you."

His words sent an unholy wave of revulsion through her. She tried to wrench free of his hold. George struck, his fist catching her in the jaw. Blood blossomed in her mouth.

"You monster!" She tried to run for the door, but he crushed her body against it before she could lift the latch.

She elbowed him hard, and he collapsed against her. She slid out from under him and rushed to the table, snatching his dinner knife. Her father's lessons hadn't included training on short blades, but she felt she could handle it if it came to it.

George spun to face her with a growl. Harriet raised the blade, feeling her father's spirit inside her like a burning flame. She would fight him with everything she had. But her throat tightened with fear as she saw the pistol. He pulled the trigger and nothing happened. She exhaled in relief, but she had only a second before he charged at her.

REDMOND STARED AT THE DISTANT GATES TO Frostmore and the black shape sitting there in between them. Devil had chased the coach all the way to the gates and then stopped, barking once or twice before he'd gone silent, still is a statue. He was waiting for Harriet to come home, and it broke Redmond's heart.

"Devil!" Redmond shouted from the front door, but the dog didn't move.

Redmond walked the distance out to the gates and stood beside his furry companion. Both of them stared down the road where Harriet had gone. Suddenly Devil spun to face the house, his hackles raised as he growled. Redmond turned as well and gasped in shock. A woman's face stared out of his bedchamber window. Even at a distance, he knew who it was.

Millicent.

"Red..." The whisper he heard was neither male nor female, and the way it caressed the air around him made him shiver.

The woman raised a hand, pressing her palm to the glass. *"Red... He has her..."*

Devil stopped growling and stood frozen, watching as the face in the window faded. The bird-song and wind blowing in from the cliffs soon came back. Only then did Redmond realize that everything had stilled while Millicent spoke to him. Her warning flashed through his mind again. His fears that the ghosts that haunted his home meant to bring him harm seemed to fade in that instant. They were warning him, helping him.

"Harriet!" He sprinted for the house, yelling for his horse.

"Your Grace?" Grindle rushed out into the hall as Redmond entered it.

"I have to go after her. She's not safe. I never should have let her go."

He ordered his horse to be made ready and went into his study to retrieve a pistol from his desk drawer and loaded it. Then he tucked it into his coat before getting on his horse. He rode for Dover, but as he reached the main road that split between Dover and Faversham as the gloom upon the land began to settle in, he saw something standing there, blocking the road to Dover.

Redmond stared at the phantom, which seemed to glow in the darkness. Redmond's lips parted, but he spoke no words. His usually gentle mare bucked wildly, as though sensing, perhaps even seeing, this supernatural vision.

Thomas.

His brother pointed toward the road leading to Faversham. His pale form glowed from a light source deep within, leaving him a ghostly pearlescent version of his former self.

"The inn..." The words had barely left Thomas's lips before he vanished.

Redmond stared down the road to Dover, where he knew Harriet had gone, but then he looked down the opposite path his brother had pointed toward. Was he losing his mind to not only see but trust these visions?

He closed his eyes, breathing deeply. He had to trust them. He steered his mount toward Faversham.

"Show me the way, brother. Show me," he pleaded upon the winds as he raced on.

He saw the distant lights of an inn ahead. A vision filled his head, clear as day. *Harriet reaching for a knife, Halifax lunging for her.* Redmond didn't waste a second as he stopped at the inn and threw the reins of his horse to a stable boy. The inside of the inn was eerily quiet. A few men sat in a corner, drinking ale over hushed whispers. They eyed him warily as he strode in. Redmond ignored them and sought the innkeeper.

"I'm looking for a man named Halifax. He may have come in with a young woman. I will pay handsomely for full information." He slapped a small purse on the counter.

The barman's eyes widened. "They were here, stayed for dinner in one of the rooms upstairs. But they started shouting, and the woman ran out toward the cliffs. The bloke went after her." The man reached for the bag of coins.

The bitter taste of panic filled Redmond's mouth. Harriet was headed for the cliffs? What was she thinking? She could fall...like Millicent.

"Where is your back door?"

The man pointed over his shoulder, through the kitchen.

"Thank you." He ran to the door, his heart pounding as he prayed that he wasn't too late.

HARRIET CLAWED GEORGE'S FACE AS HE WRESTLED her to the ground. The grass was wet with melted patches of snow. She had slipped as her boots caught on a slick spot of snow, giving George the chance to catch up with her. Now she was fighting for her life. Her body ached with the weight of him atop her.

The meager moonlight darkened the shadows on his face. He snarled and hurled himself at her. He clubbed her savagely on the temple, and she lost her hold on his hands, which now curled around her throat. She struggled for breath, trying to reach for the small knife that lay inches away from her hand. His eyes were lit with the demonic lust for death as he held her down. It would be so easy to give in, to surrender and let go. Harriet was tired of running, tired of fighting. She wanted Redmond, to be back in his arms. Her vision began to dim, and she could hear her mother's voice.

"Harriet...fight..."

He laughed heartily, the awful sound of his joy jerking her back to her senses. Her fingers touched the tip of the blade, and she strained until she curled her fingers around it. Then she swung, jabbing it deep into his side. He threw back his head and cried out in pain. His hands released her, and she punched him hard in the throat, sending him stumbling back. The instant she was free, she tried to crawl away from the cliffs, but her head swam and she nearly fainted from the pain in her skull. When she turned to see George, he was a few feet away at the cliff's edge, staring at her in fury.

"You little bitch!" He pulled the knife out and stared at her. Then his face hardened, and he stepped toward her.

Crack!

George stumbled to a stop, looking down at his chest where a dark-red spot appeared on his white shirt, growing bigger every second.

Harriet stared in stunned silence as he then stumbled back toward the edge of the cliff. A second later the dirt gave way, and he fell into the darkness below.

"Harriet?" a voice called out. She clutched her aching head and turned to see Redmond there, a pistol raised.

Redmond had shot George, had stopped him from reaching her, or else she would've fallen over the edge too. She slowly crawled backward, afraid the ground beneath her would also give way. Redmond reached her a moment later and wrapped his arms around her, carrying her away from the edge, just as he'd done two weeks ago when he'd saved her life after she'd followed a ghost to the cliffs.

"Red..." She collapsed into his arms. They both fell into the grass, holding each other.

"Are you all right?" he asked, cupping her face.

She threw her arms around his neck, and he held her long after she stopped shaking. "Yes. I am now."

The clouds parted, and a full moon shone down, casting eerie beams of light where it reflected off the snow around them.

George was gone. The monster who had kept her in fear for the last six years was no longer there to haunt her. She started to close her eyes, but then she saw it. A flickering moonbeam that for but a moment seemed to be...*Thomas*. Staring at her and Red, a sad smile hovering about his lips before the moonlight vanished behind a cloud again. The specter of George's evil in her life was ended, and for the first time in a long while, she could breathe. She felt happy, safe...and now she was with Redmond again. She marveled at how it was even possible that luck would have brought her such a fate.

"It's over," Redmond said softly. "You're safe now. He can't hurt you anymore. I'll see that the magistrate in Faversham retracts anything he might have signed about you."

"You can do that?"

"Now that Halifax is dead and I can attest to his attempt to murder you, any paperwork put before a magistrate will be suspect given the man's motives to harm you."

Harriet leaned into him, relaxing for the first time

in six years. It was over. George was gone. She was safe.

He kissed her forehead and pulled back to look down at her. "Are you ready to go home, my darling duchess?"

Harriet stared up at his handsome face, wondering how anyone could have ever thought him unattractive. He was perfect in every way.

But what had he just said? Duchess? He couldn't...

"Red, you don't have to..." He didn't need to marry her. She knew he might never again wish to marry after what had happened with Millicent. As long as she could be with him, that was all that mattered.

"You are my duchess. I thought I wasn't ready to marry again, but after almost losing you, I knew I couldn't let you out of my life again. So you'll have to marry me, Harriet. I won't have it any other way." He kissed her on the lips, a deep, sensual kiss that sent flutters through her lower belly. It banished all thoughts of the horrors she'd faced tonight, leaving only relief and joy.

"Is that so?" She felt so giddy that she couldn't resist teasing him. "Don't I have a say in this?"

Redmond smirked. "None at all. And if you resist me," he murmured seductively, "I may have to fight you for it. I'm not bad with a fencing foil."

She laughed and buried her face in his neck. "You're not terrible. But I'm better," she reminded him. "But perhaps I'll let you win."

"Would you indeed, minx?" He laughed, the cheery, open sound erasing all fear and heartache she'd suffered.

She was no longer losing him; she was going home with him.

"Come on, let's get back and hire a coach. Poor Devil may still be waiting at the gates for you."

"What?" They both stood and headed toward the distant flickering lights of the inn.

"He chased your carriage all the way to the gates and has been there ever since. He knows, like I do, that you belong at Frostmore."

"You know, he's really not a devil. Perhaps you can rename him? Angel, perhaps?"

Redmond laughed again. "He's a black guard dog. If you start calling him Angel, no one will fear him."

"Perhaps that would be a good thing?" She laughed. "For when the children come? We wouldn't want to scare the little ones."

Redmond jerked to a stop. "Children?"

She nodded, suddenly nervous. "Yes... I wanted to tell you, but then George came, and I knew I had to leave. My courses are two weeks late. I'm not certain, but"

She was unable to finish her sentence as he crushed her to his chest in a fierce hug.

"Children." He said the word with a boyish smile as he picked her up and whirled her around. When he finally set her down on her feet, he looked at her as though she was the answer to every question he'd ever had.

"Harriet. *My* Harriet." He pulled her close again. "I love you to the point of madness."

She nuzzled his throat and basked in the warmth of his body holding hers. "And I love you beyond all measure." It was a love that did not fill her with madness but rather a glorious, wondrous giddiness for life. It reminded her of when she'd been young, long before her father fell ill.

"Let's go home. We have the rest of our lives ahead of us." Redmond's voice was full of joy and hope. No more shadows, ghosts or otherwise, stood between them any longer.

"How did you know where to find me?" she asked as they reached the inn.

Redmond's eyes were serious again. "I'm not sure you'd believe me if I told you."

"Try me."

"Thomas showed me the way—after Millicent warned me you were in danger."

Harriet was quiet a long moment, thinking back to what the ghosts of Frostmore had shown her.

"I hope they can find peace together. They deserve it." She laid her head on his shoulder, and then he nodded.

"For once, I think I do as well. Frostmore shall be a place of joy from now on. A place of love and light."

"So long as we are together," she added.

"And forever beyond that." He raised her chin up to steal another kiss. Her heart was for none other than the Duke of Frostmore. He was no longer the Devil of Dover, because he had a pair of angels watching over him. And he was *her* angel.

Redmond woke to a white Christmas covering the grounds of his ancestral home. Harriet lay in his arms, still sound asleep. He almost couldn't believe how easy it had been to deal with Halifax's death. The magistrate had set aside the papers Halifax had sent him, and Harriet had been awarded Halifax's estate in its entirety since he'd had no heirs. Harriet had made mention of converting the home into a fencing school, and Redmond had agreed it was an excellent idea.

He slipped from the bed and crossed to the window while he pulled his dressing gown on. The snow stretched out as far as the eye could see, all the way to the cliffs and the deep, icy blue waters beyond. For the last seven years, the winters here had been cold and depressing. But now everything was different. The halls were full of Christmas garlands. The upstairs maids hummed carols as they cleaned. The footmen had taken the placement of kissing boughs quite seriously. More than one maid had been caught unawares for a quick giggling kiss by the young men. Frostmore was a home once again, for everyone.

Harriet stirred in bed, reaching for him. "Red?"

"Here, my darling." He rejoined her and leaned down to kiss her. She laughed in delight.

He tapped the tip of her nose. "Why don't you get dressed? It's Christmas."

She rolled her eyes. "Someone is anxious for his presents."

"I certainly am. We haven't had a proper Christmas here in seven years."

Her eyes darkened with emotions. "Oh, Red..."

He shook his head. "None of that. Now come down and meet me in the long gallery once you're dressed. I must see Grindle and Mrs. Breland and see how the preparations for tonight are coming along."

He gathered his clothes and went to change, but he took the time to steal one more kiss before he headed downstairs.

The staff were bursting with their preparations for the evening celebrations. Tonight they would be hosting a Christmas ball, where he would officially ask Harriet to be his wife.

"Grindle?" He found his butler ushering in the orchestra that would play during the event. Old friends and local families had been invited, as well as his tenant farmer families. He wanted to restart his life, to embrace being a part of the world again, thanks to Harriet. When they'd mailed out the invitations, he'd been worried that no one would come, yet the positive responses had poured in within days.

Grindle smiled broadly. "We're almost ready, Your Grace."

"Good, good." He patted his pocket nervously. It held the present he'd chosen for Harriet. "Oh, and Grindle." He caught his butler before the man left.

"Yes, Your Grace?"

"You have my permission." The confusion on Grindle's face was almost comical. "To court Mrs. Breland. Should you choose to marry, you may retain your positions here with no qualms from me."

Grindle only managed a respectful nod before rushing off to show a few straggling musicians where to set up. He was far too professional to let more than that slip past his reserve, but his thanks was clear.

A few hours later, Frostmore was full of people and music filled the house. He'd spent the hours before with Harriet as they'd talked of everything and nothing while having a late luncheon in his study. Then she'd gone back to her room to dress for the ball. Redmond greeted all his guests, including Millicent's parents.

"Your Grace," Millicent's father, Henry, greeted solemnly.

"I'm glad you came, Mr. Hubert."

Henry and his wife, Maria, both smiled a little sadly. "We're glad to be here. It's been too long." Henry proceeded into the room, but Maria remained behind.

"I hope... I hope you find happiness again, Your Grace. It's what my Millicent would've wanted." She paused, her eyes misting. "We know the rumors weren't true. We know you loved her, and we have no quarrel with you. The past is the past, and we've put it all behind us." She squeezed his hand and offered a genuine smile.

Redmond's eyes burned as he thanked Maria. He never thought that they would say that they believed him. When he'd told them of Millicent's death all those years ago, they'd left his home heartbroken, just as he had been. But he had feared, as the years passed, that they might have believed the rumors that he'd killed her. But they hadn't. They were here to celebrate Christmas, moving forward.

He cleared his throat and glanced toward the main stairs. His heart stopped. Harriet descended alone. Her satin gown was the color of ivy, and the hem and bodice were embroidered with gold ivy leaves. Her skirt split apart to reveal a red petticoat down the middle, and a thin layer of gold netting was draped over her outer skirts. Her blonde hair was pulled back, and a duchess's coronet, one that had belonged to the women of Frostmore for two hundred years, was nestled in her artful coiffure. She hadn't wanted to wear it, not until she was officially a duchess, but with a little help from Maisie, she'd been convinced to wear it. She moved as though she were in a dream. He went to her, catching her hand as she reached the last step.

"Happy Christmas, darling," he whispered as he led her to the crowd of people gathered in the hall. Then he made an announcement for everyone to follow him into the long portrait gallery. There was no formal ballroom at Frostmore, but the gallery was long and wide. Musicians inside struck up a merry waltz, and couples began to form for the first dance. Redmond pulled Harriet into his arms.

"Harriet?" he said as they began to dance beneath the candlelight.

"Yes?" She gazed at him with luminous eyes that saw into his soul.

"Marry me. Tomorrow. I have a special license from London. Marry me and become my duchess." They stopped dancing, and he pulled out the small box with his mother's ring inside, inlaid with a large brilliant ruby, surrounded by small diamonds.

"Oh, Red," she gasped. "Of course I will. Yes!"

He slipped the ring upon her finger, and the couples who had witnessed the proposal broke into applause. He held her close, wanting to kiss her, but he had caused enough of a scandal for one night.

They began to waltz again. As the couples around them joined back in, Redmond's heart caught in his throat as he recognized two figures dancing in the crowd. Their pearly luminescent glow was other-worldly as they spun between the other guests, unseen by all but him. He swallowed hard as he watched them smile and twirl before they both looked his way. His heart stopped as he recognized quite clearly their pale faces, which were full of joy. A moment later their forms transcended time itself as they faded into shimmering stardust before his eyes.

"Red? What's wrong?" Harriet asked, her worried eyes fixed on his face.

"Nothing. Everything is finally, *truly* fine." He smiled as he focused on his future wife.

If love truly was a book, then he had turned the first page, and all he saw was Harriet's face. Whatever spirits had haunted Frostmore were at peace now. And for the first time in seven years, Redmond looked toward the future instead of the past, with the love of his life dancing in his arms.

THANK YOU SO MUCH FOR READING *DEVIL AT THE Gates*! I hope you enjoyed Harriet and Redmond's love story! England was once famous for its gothic ghost stories during the yuletide season!

IF YOU LOVE A GOOD ENEMIES TO LOVERS ROMANCE, where a fortune hunter accidentally sneaks into the wrong bedroom and ends up wed to a prickly older sister of the woman he intended to marry, then you should check out my Taming of the Shrew-ish romance A *Gentleman Never Surrenders* which you can grab HERE or keep reading to see a three chapter sneak peek of bad boy Owen and his unintended bride Milly!

A GENTLEMAN NEVER
SURRENDERS

CHAPTER 1

L*ondon, October 1911*

Owen Hadley reclined in a leather armchair in one of the gaming rooms of Brooks's club on St. James Street, a glass of brandy warming his hand as he glowered at the occupants of the room. It was late in the evening and many of the old regulars of Brooks were coming in for supper. Owen's attention was only partially on the young lords gambling away their fortunes. A scowl curved his lips down as he watched the coins and pound notes changing hands.

He was in bad need of money, and the irony was not that his need arose from any vice or fault of his own. At thirty-two he was the only male heir in his family, and his estate in the Cotswolds depended on him. While he'd be away fighting a war, the land and house had fallen into disrepair and the tenant farms had been abandoned. Only a large influx of money could bring it back to life. Money he didn't have. Being merely landed gentry, land was all he had, and his was hurting.

I need a wife.

As much as he was loathe to admit it, marrying an heiress would solve the problem. But finding a woman and getting approval from her father for the match would be difficult. There were many other men, impoverished peers who could offer young ladies and their families' titles as trade for their dowries. Owen grimaced. He could offer no titles, nothing else to persuade a lady to marry him. He glanced about the other tables in the club, misery darkening his mood further.

One of the young men nearby cheered as he won a winning hand. The temporary excitement in the tame quiet of the room was grating on Owen's ears. He scowled in the direction of the exuberant gamblers. The downward movement of his lips and the tensing of his cheeks caused a bolt of pain along his bruised jaw. One week ago, he'd caught a train down to Hampton House, the country residence of his close friend Leo Graham, the Earl of Hampton.

One of the house party guests had been a divine raven-haired creature named Ivy Leighton. Her father was the owner of a London newspaper. He was nice and more importantly he was rich. The possibility of seducing the nouveau-riche newspaperman's daughter had been impossible to resist. A *very rich* young lady who would have set his home well up with her fortune. Owen had been so close to saving his estate, but he'd acted foolishly.

Perhaps a little *too* foolishly, he amended. Leo had gotten upset when he found Owen trying to steal a kiss from the young lady. Owen had been attempting to compromise her in the presence of witnesses. In such a situation, marriage would have been guaranteed, but Hampton had come upon them first and knocked Owen senseless. He still didn't understand why he and his friend, a man he'd never quarreled with before, had come to blows without warning over a woman. Owen had never felt strongly enough about any woman to throw a punch for her.

"Hadley?" A familiar voice disturbed him from his thoughts. He glanced up to see Leo staring at him with a mixture of amusement and irritation.

"Hampton," he replied, a tad gruff. He hadn't enjoyed his friend rendering him unconscious by snapping him a good blow to the jaw. It hadn't been too sporting to strike a man unawares, and Owen's pride stung a little.

"I'm glad you're here. It's been ages since we enjoyed a night at the club—"

"What do you want?" Owen growled.

"I'm sorry. I suppose I owe you an apology for hitting you. But damnation, Owen, you were in the wrong."

Owen shot him a challenging glare. "Why did you hit me? I was trying to secure myself a wife. Ms. Leighton would have been perfect for me."

"I couldn't let you have her—Ivy, I mean." Hampton lowered his voice. Speaking of a lady, even in good terms, in a club was taboo. Owen didn't care for such rules, but Leo was more of a gentleman. Ever since they were lads, Owen had always been the one more likely to get into trouble.

"Why not? Are you...interested in her?" Owen prodded, sensing there was a change in his friend. Leo seemed more...alive, like the old Leo he'd been before his father had died and the responsibilities of the estate crushed all the fun out of him.

"We were childhood friends. I hadn't seen her since she was eight, and when I met up with her again...I fell for her, *hard*. She's agreed to marry me." Leo's cheeks turned a ruddy red as he admitted this, and Owen would have laughed under other, less-tense circumstances.

So Leo was marrying the heiress? Lucky devil. *But I'm the one who really needed her.*

"I see." Owen sat back in his chair, which was close to the wall near the electric bell. He rang it and waited for the attendant. If he and Leo were going to have a discussion involving women, he needed a stiff drink.

"I should have declared my intentions toward her, Hadley. I would have, but damned if I didn't know what my intentions were until I saw you with her." Leo eased into a chair opposite Owen and nodded toward the bruised spot on Owen's face. "I'm sorry about that."

Owen's annoyance with his friend was temporarily weakened.

"I hope we can go on as we were before?" Leo inquired, his tone still low, careful. Leo was always so bloody cautious. Except when it came to Ivy Leighton, apparently. After Leo's unexpected show of violence, Owen hadn't stayed at Hampton House. He'd run back to London like a kicked dog with his tail between his legs. But their friendship ran river deep and he was not about to let a quarrel over a woman destroy that bond.

"Of course," he reassured his friend. "You can

make it up to me by finding me a rich wife," he half jested, but Leo saw through the sardonic air he'd usually cloaked his troubles with.

A servant came over with a decanter and refilled Owen's glass before offering Leo his own drink, which he accepted gratefully. After the servant left, Leo shot him a meaningful look.

Leo inched closer. "It's Wesden Heath, isn't it?"

Rather than reply, he nodded. The state of his home's affairs was dire, and thinking of it turned his stomach. And he didn't want to keep discussing his crumbling estate with his friend.

"Perhaps I can help you there. Ivy and I will be hosting another house party soon, for a Scottish lord Mother knows, someone related to her cousin I believe. Would you consider coming back for it? The Pepperwirths have just allowed their youngest daughter, Miss Rowena, to have her come-out. She's a lovely creature. Eighteen and a sizeable dowry. I know you'd do well by a wife, Hadley, so you might have a chance with her. Perhaps, if you play your hand right..." Leo trailed off, letting Owen pick up on his unspoken suggestion.

Owen sat up, confused. "Mildred Pepperwirth has a little sister?" He nearly laughed, which would have been the height of rudeness. Mildred was the eldest daughter of Viscount Pepperwirth, whose lands abutted Leo's to the west. She was a beauty, but cold and lacking in personality and warmth. The woman didn't even dance, for heaven's sake. Owen loved a woman who danced, who laughed and smiled. A woman should be happy; she should be brilliant and witty, not a cold shrew. Owen couldn't help but wonder how Rowena would compare to her sister, Mildred.

Leo's lips twitched. "She does. As I understand it, Lord Pepperwirth is very protective of Rowena and she's been quite closeted away until now. Say you'll join us and I would be happy to put in a good word for you with her father."

An attendant appeared with a tray, offering two glasses of brandy for Owen and Leo.

"Put mine on my account. I'll pay before I leave tonight," Owen informed the attendant. Once the man had left, they were relatively alone again and Owen faced his friend.

"Does Miss Rowena have any potential suitors who might throw punches too?"

Leo threw back his head in a hearty booming laugh. "Heavens, no. Though she made quite a stir during her presentation. Best if you act fast, woo the young lady before she meets any other men."

Owen sighed. "Very well, I'll come." Wooing was not a problem. He'd been wooing ladies since he was a young man. It was his lack of prospects that damaged his cause. No one wanted to marry a bloody fortune hunter, which was exactly what he was. And he hated it. Chasing women just for money left him hollow but he had no choice. His home, Wesden Heath, was sacred to him. When he'd returned from the war, scarred and broken, the wooded glens and fields of wildflowers had been his healing haven. He couldn't give it up without a fight.

"Excellent. You supping here tonight?" Leo rose from his seat.

"Planned to. You?" Owen rolled his brandy back and forth between his palms before he and Leo exited the gaming room.

"Yes, actually. I'll join you, if you don't mind the company." Leo grinned.

"Only if you tell me more of this young lady I'm to woo." Owen was relieved he and Leo were on good terms again. It wasn't at all the thing to quarrel with one's good friends. Not after everything he'd been through during the war and afterward. Good friends were worth their weight in gold and he would never forsake one, not for anything.

"Well"—Leo glanced about again, apparently determined not to be overheard—"she's quite the beauty, with flaxen hair and cornflower blue eyes..."

"WERE YOU NERVOUS, MILLY?"

Mildred Pepperwirth glanced into the mirror of her polished walnut vanity table to meet her younger sister's gaze. They were in a lavish guest room at Hampton House attending a house party through the weekend. It was the first formal dinner party in the country for her sister Rowena to attend since she'd turned eighteen.

"Nervous about what?" Milly waited patiently as their lady's maid Constance tucked the last few tendrils of Milly's chestnut hair into place. The maid had created an elegant coiffure that left a mass of hair in thick, coiled strands almost in a Grecian fashion. A green fade comb studded with diamonds was nestled in the base of her hair, keeping the intricate coils bound together.

Rowena, perched on Milly's bed, was already dressed in a white lace evening gown, one suitable for a young lady only just come out into society. She tugged on her elbow-length white gloves, fidgeting with them until she'd tugged them too tight and then was forced to loosen them again.

Milly fought off a smile. Her little sister had no reason to be nervous. She was exquisite and every male eye would be on her once she joined the other guests downstairs.

"Oh, you know. The parties, the balls, the suitors?" Rowena's eyes were soft but the same arresting shade of blue that she and Milly had inherited from their father. The brilliant color had captivated many a young man and made many a lady jealous.

"I suppose I was at first," Milly replied. "But it all becomes so tedious." She despised all the social engagements that accompanied a typical season, not because she didn't like dinners and balls or dancing. She loved to dance, loved to visit with friends, but it had only taken her one season to realize that she was nothing more than a broodmare on an auction block. The Season had only one true purpose, she'd come to realize: to secure alliances of the wealthy and elite through marriage. Milly had quickly learned to feign a distaste in dancing to avoid giving the impression she would entertain a man's romantic interest in her.

It wasn't that she didn't want to marry; she was much like any other woman—she longed for a loving husband and a happy marriage like her parents had, but she knew what her parents had was rare. They weren't simply husband and wife. They were partners in everything. From the moment her father had met her mother, they'd known they were meant to be. But Milly hadn't met a single man since her come-out who she felt that instant connection with. She wanted what her parents had. Her mother had an equal say in finances and the control of the house and their investments. Milly wanted that, too, but knew of not one single gentleman of her age who would even consider such an equality in marriage. That meant Milly had no real chance of finding a love match like they had, not one that would give her the freedom she needed.

During her years of private schooling in France, she'd been fortunate to glimpse a freer society for women, but here in England, she was a pawn, a piece to be bargained and bought, based on her family's fortune and her father's lands. The realization was unpleasant and Milly had done the only thing she could think of to avoid marriage to a stranger, or marriage to a man she couldn't stand. She'd become standoffish, mulish even, in the presence of eligible men. If they could not stand her coldness, her feigned arrogance, they left her in peace. It was a lonely peace, though, one without a hope of love. She was not brave like the suffragettes she secretly admired.

She would not have chanced such a strategy to avoid marriage if she didn't know without a doubt her father would never force her to marry. He would let her remain under his care for the rest of his life if she didn't find a man who suited her, which was her plan if she didn't find someone who could give her both freedom and happiness in a marriage. It was a lonely solution, but better than the alternative: forced to live the rest of her life with a man who would never see her full potential as a partner.

If any man viewed her as property to be bought, she could never respect him. Love could not grow in a garden sown with seeds of domestic slavery. The only way she could ever marry would be to find a man who would love her mind, her heart, and her soul and agree that she wasn't a lesser being. He would want to support her when she volunteered to teach children to read, especially girls who could benefit from education and better not only themselves but also their families. Milly needed a man who would stand beside his wife if she attended a suffragette meeting, not one who would ignore her or chastise or even forbid her from supporting her belief in equality between the sexes. But such a man did not exist, at least as far as she could tell.

Rowena got off the bed and came over to stand behind Milly, leaning down a few inches to peer at her own reflection in the mirror. She tweaked the bodice of her gown, tugging it up a little rather than down as most young ladies might.

"I don't think dancing would ever become tedious, but I am so clumsy when I'm nervous. What if I trod on my partner's toes?" Her little sister bit her bottom lip nervously.

"You'll do fine, Rowena. Stay close to me if you get nervous." Milly pinched her cheeks to pinken them a bit before she stood and reached for her black evening gloves.

"I do so love that gown," Rowena sighed.

Milly checked her figure in the full mirror by the dresser. It was a wonderful gown of sapphire blue silk with gold and black netting of lace over the bodice. The netting split apart down the front of her dress below her waist to allow the sapphire paneling to show through as she walked. The train was a little long, but the slight bustle at the back displayed her figure to its best advantage.

Constance shared a little smile with Milly as they both caught Rowena smoothing a hand over her hair before she faced them.

"How do I look?" She performed a little pirouette, her eyes shining with excitement and youth.

"You look splendid, as always." Milly clasped her little sister's hands, glad that with her sister she could be herself, if only a few minutes longer.

"Shall we go down to dinner?" she asked.

"Yes." Rowena raised her chin, a self-confidant smile replacing the girlish eagerness as though she'd become a different woman in an instant.

They departed her room, which lay in the east wing of Hampton House, where most of the guests were staying for the dinner party. A group of gentlemen and a few ladies were waiting at the bottom of the grand staircase for the other guests to come down. All eyes turned to Milly and Rowena as they came into view. Milly paused, letting Rowena have her moment to collect the admiration of the room.

Enjoy it, little sister. Someday you will have to choose your path—wife or spinster. Until she did, Rowena could enjoy her first dinner party. Milly glanced at the faces below and froze. There was one man down there she had no intention of interacting with unless forced. He hadn't been on the formal guest list but had to have been a last-minute addition. His presence wouldn't have stopped her from coming, but lord she so hated to be around men like him...After the last house party at Hampton House, she'd been determined to avoid him if possible.

Mr. Owen Hadley was a fortune hunter. A man like that was dangerous. They cared little or not at all for the women they seduced in an attempt to find suitable heiresses. She stared hard at the man's face for a moment longer, wishing she could will him to disappear. But he stayed right where he was, his presence mocking her for her inability to make him vanish.

His scandalous reputation preceded him, and he left a trail of broken hearts and unmarried ladies who lacked the wealth it was rumored he was seeking behind him. She'd heard far too much about Hadley's history with women. How he'd worked his way into many beds, but the widowed ladies knew better than to marry him. A rich widow had the world at her fingertips, and very rarely did those ladies remarry, because it meant turning over their freedom and money to their new husbands. Milly had to applaud those widows for turning the fortune hunter away. Mr. Hadley was a temptation to sin for any woman.

Even Milly had to admit that as he stood there in his evening suit, dark hair long enough to look a tad too roguish to be fashionable, and that grin that melted a woman's resistance, he looked good. He was tall, *too tall*, but perfect for her, not that she liked that—she *didn't*, of course. She preferred to be an equal height to men, and given that she possessed a little more height than many young ladies, most men of her acquaintance weren't taller than her. Hadley, however, was too tall, almost a head above Milly. It made her feel...vulnerable.

Hadley laughed at something the Earl of Hampton said and then glanced up the stairs. His eyes flicked over her briefly, a hint of a frown touching his sensual lips; then his focus turned to Rowena and damn him, the man's hazel eyes lit up with a piercing fire.

Milly's stomach clenched and she froze on the stairs, one gloved hand clasped to her breast.

Rowena. Not her sweet Rowena. The man could seduce any lady, but not her little sister. Rowena needed a good match. Scandal would ruin her beyond redemption and she would be forced out of polite society.

I will have to distract him, even if it will be most distasteful.

Squaring her shoulders, Milly walked down the last two steps and greeted her hosts. The Dowager Countess of Hampton; her soon-to-be-husband, Mr. Leighton; and his daughter, Ivy, along with Leo Graham, the Earl of Hampton.

"You look splendid," Ivy said as she took Milly's arm.

Milly never failed to be surprised at Ivy Leighton's friendliness. The young woman was half Gypsy by her father, and her mother had been a lady's maid. It was in every instinct Milly possessed to treat Ivy coolly given her status as nouveau riche, which happened to be below Milly's own long-generation titled lineage. The first time they'd been introduced, Milly had certainly acted unpleasant. She regretted that. *Immensely*. Her frustration with Leo's intent to propose to her had put a damper on her mood. Milly had been so focused on convincing the earl that she wasn't a good match for him that she'd acted rather callously and arrogantly with regard to everyone around her. Ivy had been a victim of her behavior, and in the last few weeks Milly had made every effort to be deserving of the friendship that Ivy offered.

Ivy had been persistent, and Milly had found herself unable to dislike the young woman once they'd spent a few afternoon teas together discussing literature and politics. They had much in common in their views with regard to women and the rights they unfairly lacked in society.

Milly tilted her head close to Ivy to whisper, "What is Mr. Hadley doing here? As I understood it, he and Lord Hampton had a falling out at the last house party." It had been quite a scandal. Mr. Hadley had left during the middle of a shooting party with a black eye and a sour temper.

Milly allowed Ivy to guide her away from the other guests into an alcove where they could have a small amount of privacy. Ivy's bright caramel eyes darkened a little.

"I'm not sure, but Leo insists they are still friends

and that Mr. Hadley no longer has intentions of trying to steal me from Leo."

Milly huffed in reply. "Of course he doesn't, because he's eyeing my sister like a fine glass of sherry he wants to taste." She glowered at the accused seducer, hoping that he could feel the sting of her gaze. He turned and raised one brow in challenge at her from across the room.

"Milly," Ivy gasped, but it soon turned to a giggle as she followed Milly's fixed attention.

"He does look a little too interested. It's a good thing the seating arrangement at dinner keeps him away from Rowena."

Milly touched her throat as she readjusted the diamond necklace that lay against her collarbone. "Who's the unfortunate party guest that must endure his conversation?"

Ivy shot her a sideways glance. "Why you, Milly dear."

For a moment, Milly simply couldn't process what her friend had just told her. She'd been resolved to distract him from Rowena but that didn't include seating next to the odious man at dinner.

"Absolutely no—" Milly was silenced as the butler announced dinner was prepared. "Ivy, I'm not sitting next to that man," she hissed in her friend's ear.

Ivy merely laughed. "Someone has to and who

better than you? I think you're a perfect match in ill tempers." The teasing comment made Milly frown deeply. Even though she'd been seemingly ill-tempered on purpose, it wasn't who she really was. Deep down, she was a woman who wanted love and laughter in her life. But a man like Hadley would never see the real her, nor would a man like him want a real partner in life. He only wanted a wife for money. He embodied everything she hated.

CHAPTER 2

The ladies went from the drawing room to the lavish dining room first. Milly blanched as she went to her seat. A footman stepped out of the shadows, pulled her chair back, and seated her. She felt like a man doomed to die by hanging, waiting on the scaffold for the quick drop and the final stop. She had to deal with Mr. Hadley. There was something unsettling about being too close to him, the scent of sandalwood and pine that she caught as she stood only a few feet away from him, and the way his lips curved up in a wry smile as she came closer. It made her knees buckle and her pulse pound. Nothing about Mr. Hadley made her feel stable and in control.

Still, it was better that she do it than Rowena. Her younger sister might fall for the dark-haired seducer with his devilish smiles and hearty laughter. Yes, it was a good thing Rowena was seated closer to the quiet and handsome Scottish Earl of Forres. He was a much safer dinner companion than a fortune hunter like Hadley.

"Miss Pepperwirth," Mr. Hadley greeted coldly as he took a seat beside her once all the ladies and remaining gentlemen had taken their seats.

"Good evening, Mr. Hadley," she replied just as coolly. By the end of the third course, they'd likely frost their end of the table over with their chilled politeness.

"Are you enjoying the weather?" His question surprised her, and she answered before thinking through her response.

"The weather? It is October, Mr. Hadley, a lovely autumnal month. Of course I enjoy it." She hadn't meant to say that, hadn't meant to reveal anything about herself that she enjoyed. It made her likeable, and that meant suitors would notice her. She couldn't allow that.

"You enjoy October, then? What about it do you like?" He dipped his spoon into his bowl of cream of watercress soup and then after tasting it, angled his body toward her. It was inappropriate to do so, but no one else seemed to notice his position or his focus on her.

His eyes met hers and she saw a challenging gleam in his gaze underlaid with other more confusing emotions...heat, but not anger. She met him stare for stare despite the fact that his gaze made her feel as naked as though she wore nothing more than a corset and chemise.

A sudden flush heated Milly's body from the tips of her toes to her cheeks. How could a simple move, his body turned toward her in a close setting, make her react so...strongly?

Like a fever. The thought only just penetrated the haze that lingered at the edge of her mind and body. She brought herself out of it with a little shake of her head.

"I'm sorry, what did you ask me?" For the life of her she couldn't remember his question.

"October, what do you like about it?" He was blatantly ignoring the woman on his right and a few people across the table were noticing.

Milly swallowed hard and reached for her water goblet. Her tongue felt a little thick and her throat dry. Hadley's intense focus on her was unsettling.

"I...uh...enjoy the changing of the colors of the leaves, the way the crisp breeze has a slight bite to it."

Oh dear, I'm rambling. She hastily took a few sips of her watercress soup, not daring to look in Hadley's direction. When he said nothing, she finally was forced to look his way. Those eyes, the ones that promised danger and seduction, were entirely fixed on her. How could he make her feel so naked and excited? As though she had no secrets from him and with that glint of arrogance she saw, he knew *exactly* what she was thinking. She stared back at him, her heart thumping hard enough that she wondered if her ribs would be bruised on the morrow.

"And you, Mr. Hadley. What do you like about October?"

He chuckled. "I don't like the month. Not at all. I prefer June or July. The heat, you know, I like that much better. The feel of the sun warming my bare skin...a man can grow addicted to the feel of that pleasurable burning, perhaps even a woman can, too."

The heat? He liked the heat? She very much doubted that he meant the heat of the sun. No, she sensed that the heat he referred to was something else entirely, something she wasn't supposed to know about, being a virgin, and yet she did. She only knew enough to know it was bad to think of words like *heat* and *pleasurable burning* in such a scandalous fashion. There was something about the way he said the words and how his eyes darkened as he looked at her that made it feel so wrong. So wrong in a delicious way like eating the last bit of dessert when she'd already had too much.

"You don't like the heat?" Owen finally broke his stare and turned to face his bowl of soup again.

With his concentration on her disrupted, Milly's strength returned. "No. I most certainly do not."

With a practiced ease, Mr. Hadley tossed one shoulder in a casual shrug and replied,

"Pity, it might have been fun for you and I to enjoy the summer heat together." And then he didn't converse with her for the remainder of the dinner.

For some reason, it made her angry, angry and a little hurt. Which made no sense, since she didn't like him. Despised him, in fact. Then why did it sting? She shouldn't want him to continue talking to her or discussing things that were likely far too scandalous for dinner, but there had been something to him when he spoke to her. She'd felt...alive even as they'd played whatever sort of game he'd started and she missed the feeling of excitement that came with verbally sparring with him, even for so short a time.

For the remainder of the meal, she partook minimally in the other conversations, still mulling over Owen's words and what they really meant...and more importantly how his heated gaze had made her feel.

After dinner, Milly spent the remainder of the evening, while the men were unaware, speaking with Ivy about joining the local suffragettes for their meetings. If Milly was to remain unwed, she wanted to devote her life to her passion—the education of women—and Ivy had some wonderful ideas of how Milly could become involved. It left her feeling full of hope for the first time in years. She would have a purpose, one not buried by society's expectations but rather one that would challenge her and give young girls a sense of a future that was bright and filled with chances they would never have dreamed of without proper education.

It was a long while later when the ladies were finally ready to go to bed. The gentlemen had gone to drink port in another part of the large manor house and the ladies of the party were thankfully in agreement that it was time to retire.

Milly joined Rowena as they ascended the main set of stairs and walked down the hall to their wing. Their rooms were opposite each other in the hall.

"Rowena, remember to lock your door after Constance sees to you," she reminded her little sister.

"My door...why of course, but why would you tell me to?" Rowena entered her chamber, where Constance stood waiting. Pinching her earrings off and her delicate diamond bracelets, she handed them to their maid, who carried them over to a sateen jewelry box on the dresser.

"It's Mr. Hadley. I don't like the way he was looking at you tonight." Milly leaned against one of the bedposts, gripping the wood between her gloved hands.

"How was he looking at me? What do you mean, Milly?" Her little sister's eyes were wide and a little fearful.

"You're too young to know what sort of man he is, but trust me when I say you don't want to be someone he is interested in. Fortune hunters are heartless. They only care about the money they can get when they ruin you. I saw the way he was looking at you tonight. I believe he might try to seduce you. You could not survive the scandal if he did. You must take care not to be anywhere alone, especially with him. After dinner tonight, I was worried he might try to visit your rooms. It is the easiest way to compromise a woman."

At this her sister froze, her gown half undone in the back. Constance even paused in the act of slipping buttons of their slits.

"He'll try to compromise me?"

Milly sighed. Her sister was so innocent, like a sacrificial lamb.

"Yes. He'd compromise you. Come to your chambers in nothing but a dressing gown, climb into your bed, and arrange to be discovered with you." Milly paused. She wasn't all that sure of what followed except there might be a fair amount of kissing and something about a man lying atop a woman.

"Oh, Milly, you mean you think he'd..." Rowena made a funny little gesture with her hands by squishing them together almost as if she were in prayer.

Milly nodded. "He would force himself on you."

Rowena gasped.

It was a fate worse than death in Milly's eyes. Being compromised and then forced to marry the man who ruined you. Men who did that to women didn't love them, and a marriage without love was something she never wanted to contemplate.

"My lady." Constance flashed Milly a panicked look because Rowena had turned a frightening ashen white. Milly grasped her sister by the shoulders, giving her a gentle shake.

"Rowena, I'm so sorry. I didn't mean to frighten you. I'm sure Mr. Hadley wouldn't hurt you. He seems only to break hearts, not other things. I do not believe he'd do any real harm, except to your reputation. But you must take care all the same. Lock your door."

When her sister nodded, her eyes still as round as teacup saucers, Milly kissed her cheek and then left to cross the hall to her own room to prepare for bed. She unfastened her necklace and removed her earrings before she slid her black gloves off and laid them down over the back of a chair. She would have to wait for Constance to assist her, so she seated herself at the vanity table. What a night she'd had, suffering Mr. Hadley's strange behavior at dinner. Had he meant to tease her the way a cat did a mouse? It seemed likely he'd only attempted conversation with her out of boredom.

A pity that, she thought. *I would have loved to have a genuine conversation with anyone, even him.* But all the things she longed to discuss, like politics or history, were not favorable topics for a lady to discuss. In France, she'd been able to speak so freely to men about her opinions. Back in England she'd been forced to accept the fact that the life she'd been living in France would likely never be possible here. Men still wished to go to separate rooms to smoke, leaving women to their idle gossip. She knew Ivy and Leo broke from tradition frequently and would sit and talk for hours about things that *mattered*.

I wish I could have that. The longing for it was so desperate that it left her feeling empty and cold because she feared she would never find a man who would wish to do that with her.

For a moment, she thought of Owen's flashing dark eyes and the way he'd riled her temper up as they'd talked but how he'd also made her feel things she hadn't ever felt before.

Heat. The word he'd used to tease her seemed to make her entire body burn at the thought. If she had to be completely honest with herself, his teasing had been enjoyable. But admitting that made her frown. He was a fortune hunter and she shouldn't enjoy his attentions. Of course, she had no reason to worry; he had no real interest in her.

Men like him, while they loved the challenge of seducing women, wouldn't be overly interested in someone like her, not when easy prey like her little sister was available. Envy slithered beneath her skin in that moment and she wished, at least some small part of her did, that Owen wanted her, not Rowena. It was foolish, nonsensical, but part of her longed to be desired. But it didn't matter; she was in no danger of ever being married at this rate, nor would she ever be the subject of a fortune hunter's seductions. She'd developed her prickly exterior too well to stop even the most determined man from trying to woo her. But that didn't stop her from wanting the right man, the one who would love her, to see through her façade.

Milly was still brooding when Constance entered her bedchamber and came over to help her undress. After the layers of silk dropped to the floor and her corset and chemise were removed, Constance held out a long, comfortable, elegant nightdress with fine lace trimmed with ribbon inserts. Milly tugged her hair into a loose rope to one side and plucked a blue ribbon from her jewelry case and tied it in a bow around her hair at the nape of her neck.

"Ready for bed, milady?" Constance asked as she turned down Milly's bed.

"Yes," she replied, extremely weary.

She'd been up since dawn, helping Rowena prepare for the social niceties that would occur tonight and on future nights during her first Season. Rowena had been understandably concerned that she would make a mistake tonight. She hadn't, of course; she had behaved beautifully. Milly could not have been prouder of her. The handsome Earl of Forres, who'd traveled all the way from Scotland for this house party, had even shown an interest in Rowena. According to Ivy, Forres was recently widowed and the father of a beautiful two-year-old daughter he'd brought down to England. He and his daughter had stayed here for a few weeks with the Dowager Countess of Hampton, who was some distant relation of his.

"I'll come check on you in the morning when I bring your tea and scones." Constance smiled and took her leave.

Milly climbed onto the bed and pulled the bedclothes up around her chest and sighed. The bed was so large, and rather lonely. Usually she didn't let such a melancholy thought bother her, but tonight for some reason, it did. There was a dull ache in her chest and she rubbed the spot with her hand. Somewhere tonight, Mr. Hadley was likely climbing into bed, dreaming of all the young ladies' hearts he would steal and break. A treacherous little flutter in her chest made Milly wince. She ought not to think of Hadley, certainly not while she was in bed...yet thinking of him, as frustrating and maddeningly irritating as he was, flushed her with a welcome heat in the chilly room.

The oil lamp beside her bed was the only light left in the room and it burned steadily. Often she read late into the night and forgot to turn it off, but tonight she was too tired to read. She reached over and gently twisted the brass knob to kill the little flame. Darkness absorbed the dying light and Milly flipped onto her back. The cold of the sheets almost stung her bare toes and legs when her nightdress rode up to her knees. A cold bed, an empty bed. It shouldn't have upset her, but after Mr. Hadley's talk of heat and summer, she was off balance and bothered.

The mere thought of him and the way his eyes

had darkened and seemed to shimmer with inner flames brought on another rush of warmth. His eyes, like honeyed fire, and his lips, the way he'd smiled sardonically, almost mockingly, in a way she rather liked, irritated her, yet fascinated her. There was no reason to like a man's mouth or to imagine what it might be like to have that mouth pressed to hers in a kiss that caused the heat he was so fond of discussing. She knew his kiss would be hot, because when she thought of it, her body blossomed with a swelling of heat in her belly. *His mouth is wicked...sinful...and I hate that I wish to know how he tastes.* It was a forbidden thought, but one she couldn't deny. She rolled over onto her stomach, fluffed her pillow, and squeezed her eyes shut, attempting to will herself to sleep. It was going to be a long night.

CHAPTER 3

Owen paced the length of his bedchamber, wearing light trousers and a dressing gown, but no shirt. His valet, Evans, had come and gone, having helped him undress and put away neckcloths, cuff links, and a hundred other minor details of Owen's wardrobe. Normally he and Evans would converse at length on any number of topics but tonight he had one thing on his mind.

Rowena Pepperwirth.

Such a lovely young lady and perfect for his needs. Even though he hadn't had a chance to speak with her that evening, he'd seen enough to know he'd happily bed her. He'd asked Evans tonight to discern where his future bride was sleeping. Apparently, she was in the opposite wing, just past the suit of armor on the left.

Owen checked the clock on the marble mantel-piece above the fireplace in his chamber. Half-past midnight. Surely she was asleep by now. All he needed to do was slip inside her chamber and wait to be "discovered" when Evans found a reason to have Rowena's mother come to check on her. Stalking over to the door, he cracked it open and peered into the hall. Empty. No servants were within sight and no houseguests either.

He slipped out of his bedroom and hastily took the route Evans had described. The golden light of the hall lamps and the rich red carpet made the hall feel warm and cheery. It put him in good spirits. This plan was going to work. He paused at reaching the chain-mail knight. His reflection in the shiny helmet was almost comical and he smiled. After tonight his future would be secured; he would have a lovely young bride and Wesden Heath would have a fortune to sustain it. He just hated that he had to secure his home by such dastardly means. He'd tried wooing widows and heiresses the last year with no success. Desperation had driven him to this foolish scheme but he couldn't turn back.

Two more steps and he was facing Rowena's door: the woman who would become his wife, albeit through scandalous measures. But Wesden Heath needed to be protected and supported.

"You've got this, old boy," he muttered in encouragement, and reached for the door handle. The latch clicked down and the door pushed inward to the darkened room.

Good. She was asleep. Padding softly into the room, he closed the door behind him. It was impossible to see except for the sliver of light cutting through the thick baize curtains in front of the window. Eventually his eyes adjusted to the lack of light and he made out a bed against one wall. Walking carefully over to the window, he swept a hand between the curtains, pushing them apart. Milky moonlight now bathed the bed and its occupant enough to tease Owen with a view of a languidly stretched body with healthy curves. Bedding Rowena once they were married would be a most enjoyable experience, and he would teach the innocent young lady how to seek her own pleasure, too. He wanted his marriage bed to be full of mutual desire and ecstasy. A woman who was well loved in bed made a happy woman out of bed. And he planned to see to his future wife's happiness once they'd settled in at Wesden Heath.

Rowena shifted in the bed, sighed, and kicked one leg free of her blankets. Silky white skin made his fingers ache to stroke up from her delicate ankle to her upper thigh. Lord, the temptation to touch her, to take what he wanted, was so strong, but he mastered his control. Rowena suddenly rolled restlessly in his direction and then she gasped.

"Who are you?" Her voice was a panicked whisper.

"It is me, Owen, Hadley. I've come to—"

"Mr. Hadley?" The outrage in her tone was surprisingly forceful and her voice was deeper than he remembered, a sensual huskiness of a grown woman, rather than a young woman of eighteen.

"Rowena." He paused, unsure of what to say, but she sat bolt upright in bed and fumbled with the wooden nightstand. A rasp of a match and then an oil lamp bloomed, casting a light on the woman in his bed.

"Good God," he cursed.

Mildred, not Rowena, glowered at him, her long dark chestnut hair in a luscious tangle of wild waves about her shoulders. For a moment, he was utterly distracted by the thought of threading his fingers through her hair as he tilted her head back for a kiss.

"Mr. Hadley, leave my chamber at once before someone sees you." Mildred only then seemed to realize her nightdress had ridden up her legs and she tugged it down before she slid out of bed. The fabric clung to her more than she expected it to.

"Please, Mr. Hadley."

Her plea broke through the haze of his building curiosity and desire.

*Right, Mildred, must leave now...*Sanity restored itself in rapid fire and he headed for the door. The moment his hand touched the knob, he had to stumble back as it opened. A lady's maid with a shawl about her shoulders and a lamp in one hand froze upon seeing him.

"My lady...," the woman murmured in a hushed sound of shock.

The situation was far worse than Owen could have predicted. Lady Pepperwirth in her dressing gown and hair unbound, stood just behind the maid, her keen eyes sweeping over Owen and the scene with surprise.

"Constance said she was informed you'd taken ill, Milly dear," Lady Pepperwirth said, but her frown said everything her words did not. "It seems it is not an illness that plagues you, but something else."

"Mama, Mr. Hadley came here by mistake. He was just leaving—"

Lady Pepperwirth entered the room and motioned for Constance to come in as well.

"Silence, Milly. The damage is done. The four of us know what has happened tonight, but we cannot let word spread or else we will have a serious problem." Lady Pepperwirth turned on Owen. "You, Mr.

Hadley, will ask for Milly's hand tomorrow by speaking with my husband. I will tell him he should accept and the wedding will be done within a few weeks. If anyone asks, you two have had a secret understanding the last year and are now to be married. Is that understood?"

Owen sputtered. "I..."

"You'll be properly compensated, Mr. Hadley. My eldest daughter's dowry is far larger than Rowena's is."

Could the viscountess read his mind?

"That is what you were concerned about, was it not?" Lady Pepperwirth's chilly stare almost made him flinch.

Owen cleared his throat and nodded. "I will be honored to ask for Miss Pepperwirth's hand first thing tomorrow."

"Good. Now, I suggest we all retire for the night. Many preparations will need to be made on the morrow." Lady Pepperwirth opened the door and nudged a still-stunned Constance out into the hallway.

For a long moment, Owen couldn't move. His mind was blank and he felt as though his feet were rooted to the carpet.

"What have you done?" Mildred hissed.

Her chiding tone got under his skin and he spun to face her.

"I've gotten us engaged, that's what I've done, and we cannot get out of it." He shoved his hands into his robe's pockets, fuming.

Mildred walked right up to him and jabbed a finger into his bare chest through the parted robe.

"You thought I was Rowena. It was her you meant to compromise, wasn't it?"

He grasped her wrist, but rather than push her hand away, he held on to it, admiring the soft, warm skin beneath his hand. Her pulse raced wildly at that delicate point on her inner wrist where his fingers curled around it.

I should let go. But he didn't. He was staring at her bright blue eyes so full of fire and those soft rosebud lips in a pout that made him want to kiss them, perhaps take a nibble...

"Hadley, are you listening to me?" She struggled to free her wrist from his hand.

"Mildred, please, call me Owen. We are to be married." He tried to bite back a sudden smile at the entire ridiculous situation. Neither of them had wanted this, and he felt damned awful for upsetting Mildred. It was clear she didn't want to be married and while he didn't exactly like her, at least in the traditional sense, he didn't want to upset her. The honest truth was he had destroyed both their lives, but more so hers than his. He'd been ready to marry a stranger—and it was clear Mildred was not—and he hated causing her the pain that he saw in her eyes despite her rising ire.

He wasn't sure if it was a nightmare to be married to her or not. He would have to wait and find out. There was something undeniably fascinating about riling Mildred's temper. Even if he was condemned to marry the harpy, he could at least laugh about it.

"Fine. Owen. And if you call me Mildred again, I'll…"

His lips twitched. "You prefer Milly, then? So do I. Thank heavens we agree on one thing at least."

Her feminine huff of displeasure made him chuckle. Just like October and July. They were opposites. What a dreadful match they would make. Yet, since he was doomed, he might as well embrace the absurdity of knowing he would be marrying her in a few weeks.

"You've ruined everything!" Milly snapped, but he saw the glimmer of hurt in her eyes rather than anger. Had she loved another? Was he robbing her of a man she'd intended to marry?

"Milly, did you…" He swallowed before continuing. "Did you have an understanding with another man?" Why he wanted her to say no he wasn't sure.

The thought of her weeping into a pillow over someone else after she became his was not a pleasant thought, not that he wanted her. He didn't. He wanted Rowena.

Milly sighed, a little tear dripping down her right cheek as she pulled her wrist free of his grasp. She walked around him to her bed and sat on the edge, tucking her knees up under her chin like a child.

"I didn't want to marry anyone, not like this..." She sniffed and looked up at him. "And now I'm to be stuck with you." She waved a hand at him and then sniffed again, her eyes too bright, too full of tears. Had he ever believed Milly Pepperwirth capable of crying? No, he hadn't. She'd always been this bastion of female spinsterdom to him. Beautiful, but cold and untouchable. Who was this teary-eyed beauty who lit an unwelcome yet undeniable fire in his blood?

He was moving before he was aware of it. He eased down beside her on the bed and cupped her chin, turning her face toward his.

"Milly, I'm sorry I've done this to you, to both of us." He meant it. They were stuck with each other and it was his fault. She didn't deserve this fate and he was a coward for compromising her like this and forcing her into it. The hard lump in his throat made it hard to breathe for a moment.

Her long lashes fluttered, tears coating her lips

like tiny crystals. This wasn't the angry woman from dinner earlier that evening; this woman was vulnerable and oddly beautiful despite her eyes reddened with tears. His chest tightened as he faced the fact that he had made her weep. Owen couldn't help but wonder if her aloof act was truly that, *an act*.

"Then don't go see my father tomorrow. Just leave. I'll not tell a soul what happened."

He shook his head. "The damage is done." He shifted a few inches closer, his hand on her chin sliding around to cup her cheek. Her skin was soft as silk and he half closed his eyes as he fixed on her lips. He had the sudden urge to taste her, a woman he couldn't stand.

"Let me kiss you," he begged in a ragged whisper. Swept away by a surge of desire, he wanted to taste this woman's lips to see how fiery she was when she wasn't verbally sparring with him.

"What?" She blinked in surprise and drew back an inch.

Every predatory instinct in him took over and he dipped his head, brushing his lips over hers, light enough for her to still withdraw or to lean forward. Her mouth trembled against his and he felt her lean in, just a bare quarter inch. He curled his fingers around the back of her neck and held her still for his plundering kiss. He tasted her, teased her lips, and stroked the tip of his tongue along the seam of her mouth. A soft little throaty sound escaped Milly and he wanted to crow in triumph as she kissed him back. The lady could be seduced after all!

It took a surprising amount of willpower for him to separate their mouths. He rested his forehead against hers and stroked her cheeks with his thumbs as they shared panting breaths.

"I know this isn't what you wanted, and I am sorry." He kissed her again, this time on her cheek, and exited the room before she could say another word or shed another tear that he would see.

Want to know what happens next? Grab Owen and Milly's story HERE!

Historical

The League of Rogues Series

Wicked Designs

His Wicked Seduction

Her Wicked Proposal

Wicked Rivals

Her Wicked Longing

His Wicked Embrace

The Earl of Pembroke

His Wicked Secret

The Last Wicked Rogue

Never Kiss A Scot

The Earl of Kent

Never Tempt a Scot (coming 2020)

The Seduction Series

The Duelist's Seduction

The Rakehell's Seduction

The Rogue's Seduction

The Gentleman's Seduction

Standalone Stories

Tempted by A Rogue

Bewitching the Earl

Seducing an Heiress on a Train

Devil at the Gates

Sins and Scandals

An Earl By Any Other Name

A Gentleman Never Surrenders

A Scottish Lord for Christmas

Contemporary

The Surrender Series

The Gilded Cuff

The Gilded Cage

The Gilded Chain

The Darkest Hour

Love in London

Forbidden

Seduction

Climax

Forever Be Mine

Paranormal

Dark Seductions Series

The Shadows of Stormclyffe Hall
The Love Bites Series
The Bite of Winter
His Little Vixen (coming early 2020)
Brotherhood of the Blood Moon Series
Blood Moon on the Rise (coming soon)
Brothers of Ash and Fire
Grigori: A Royal Dragon Romance
Mikhail: A Royal Dragon Romance
Rurik: A Royal Dragon Romance

Sci-Fi Romance
Cyborg Genesis Series
Across the Stars
The Krinar Chronicles
The Krinar Eclipse
The Krinar Code by Emma Castle

Buy these books today by visiting www.
laurensmithbooks.com
Or by visiting your favorite ebook/paperback book
store!

ABOUT THE AUTHOR

Lauren Smith is an Oklahoma attorney by day, author by night who pens adventurous and edgy romance stories by the light of her smart phone flashlight app. She knew she was destined to be a romance writer when she attempted to re-write the entire *Titanic* movie just to save Jack from drowning. Connecting with readers by writing emotionally moving, realistic and sexy romances no matter what time period is her passion. She's won multiple awards in several romance subgenres including: New England Reader's Choice Awards,

Greater Detroit BookSeller's Best Awards, and a Semi-Finalist award for the Mary Wollstonecraft Shelley Award.

To Connect with Lauren, visit her at:
www.laurensmithbooks.com
lauren@laurensmithbooks.com
Facebook Fan Group - Lauren Smith's League
Lauren Smith's Newsletter

Never miss a new release! Follow me in one or more of the ways below!

f facebook.com/LaurenDianaSmith

y twitter.com/LSmithAuthor

O instagram.com/Laurensmithbooks

BB bookbub.com/authors/lauren-smith

Made in the USA
Monee, IL
20 August 2023

41299306R00152